WAVE FORMS AND DOOM SCROLLS

ALSO BY DANIEL SCOTT TYSDAL

Fauxccasional Poems
The Mourner's Book of Albums
*Predicting the Next Big Advertising Breakthrough
Using a Potentially Dangerous Method*
The Writing Moment: A Practical Guide to Creating Poems

WHAT IS MISSING

YEAR ZERO

HUMANITY'S WING

WAVE FORMS <u>AND</u>

THE POEM

WAVE FORM

DEAR ADOLF

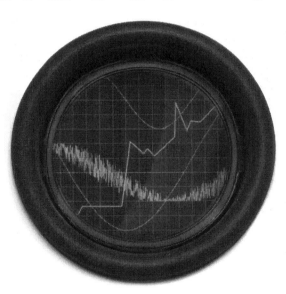

1 DOG, 1 KNIFE

DOOM SCROLLS

POEMB

DOOM SCROLLS

BOOMING

STORIES

DANIEL SCOTT

TYSDAL

A BUCKRIDER BOOK

Published by Buckrider Books
an imprint of Wolsak and Wynn Publishers
280 James Street North
Hamilton, ON L8R2L3
www.wolsakandwynn.ca

Editor: Paul Vermeersch | Copy editor: Ashley Hisson
Cover and interior design: Michel Vrana
Cover image: created using images from iStockphoto
Author photograph: Andrea Charise
Typeset in Adobe Caslon Pro, Futura, Trade Gothic
Printed by Rapido Books, Montreal, Canada

Printed on certified 100% post-consumer Rolland Enviro Paper.

10 9 8 7 6 5 4 3 2 1

The publisher gratefully acknowledges the support of the Ontario Arts Council, the Canada Council for the Arts and the Government of Canada.

Library and Archives Canada Cataloguing in Publication

Title: Wave forms and doom scrolls : stories / Daniel Scott Tysdal.
Names: Tysdal, Daniel Scott, 1978- author.
Identifiers: Canadiana 20210257210 | ISBN 9781989496381 (softcover)
Classification: LCC PS8639.Y84 W38 2021 | DDC C813/.6—dc23

for Jayne and Nathan
with thanks for your love
and love of story

before dust chokes the single outline,
blurs the individual mouth.
— Kay Smith, "You in the Feathery Grass"

isityouinthevideo.com
— Twenty-First-Century Adage

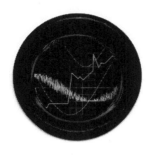

CONTENTS

WHAT IS MISSING

THE NIGHT AFTER THE BOY WAS KIDNAPPED A GROUP
of teens got high and formed the Ministry of Pre-Emptive
Memorials. The Minister of Stuffed Animals, the Minister of
Flowers and the Minister of Signed Letters and Anonymous
Poems embarked with the others in pairs to locate the goods
they'd been assigned to gather. Their work was finished by dawn,
and they photographed it, though the memorial lacked the contribution of the Minister of Wreaths, who had been arrested lurking
naked in the meat section of an all-night supermarket. The memorial did not bear witness to the boy. What the friends had prepared
was meant to brace the world against a calamity yet to come. To
keep it ready.

But the next morning a woman who had knit a toque for the
kidnapped boy mistook these flowers piled with crucifixes and
homemade cards as a gathering undertaken for him; she added
her offering. She had seen footage from the mall's security camera, on TV first, then online, and it doesn't look like a kidnapping.

A figure emerges from the crowd of holiday shoppers. They share a few exchanges, man and boy, and then vanish down a hall, hand in hand. A comment posted online describes the uncoloured blur of their encounter as two ghosts in the afterlife meeting again for the first time. The woman only knew how to knit toques, which was fine; the days were getting shorter. She promised the boy if she learned to knit mitts she would leave a pair to match the hat.

The boy's father had already destroyed the memorial created for his missing child. Neighbours had started it at the entrance of a local park. The boy's father shredded hand-drawn laments and snapped stems as he shouted, "He isn't dead!" Gathering the debris into a pile, he ignited it using gas from a jerry can and his car's cigarette lighter.

The boy's father also had reservations about the candlelit vigil organized by their church, but he was too busy keeping pressure on the police to imagine the proper protest. His wife spent the whole vigil onstage, though she wasn't really there. Eyes closed on the encouragement each speaker extended to the crowd, eyes closed on the glow of the crowd's flickering support, the boy's mother did what she could to keep close to her son. She sent herself into him. If it had to be this way, it had to; she alone in her love would be the last thing he sensed or saw.

In the passing days, she kept this up, increased her efforts tenfold, even as she and her husband held press conferences, gave interviews to reporters and local talk-show hosts. Their boy became a lesson to other children – the don'ts and dos of strangers. Many of these children, this ancient tale new in their ears, wondered what it would be like to be the boy's friend or cousin or sibling or – their stomachs twisting at the thought of it – what would it be like to be that, taken away? A pastor told the story of Christ's empty tomb and said the boy, like that abandoned burial, reminds us of the power of what is missing. One parishioner wondered if this reminder was worth the boy's loss before deciding it was; as the pastor said, the boy teaches us to hope. He will be found. It all will have been for the best.

By then the boy was dead. The death had not been a part of the kidnapper's plan. Before finding the boy, the kidnapper had taken pictures of different spaces in his own home. He had secretly poured over the photos at work, trying to decide where in his house the boy would live. To him, great men coined new absences, removed whole peoples, their paces, from the world's endless racing. The room had been right. The boy had not. He would never be a great man but that was okay. Soon he would find another boy. Soon he would find another time to take another life and hold it. Soon, in another room, if need be.

Soon the boy was gone from the headlines, gone from small talk, gone from all the streams and feeds. Other events overtook him. The sun's rays grew more dangerous. Rebels barricaded themselves in a classroom of first graders. A stewardess birthed mid-flight a little one she wasn't even aware she'd conceived. One octogenarian, though, did wake in the night months later with the urge to pray for the safety of that poor kidnapped boy she had read about in the news. She pushed through the papers piled in the kitchen, searching for something with his name. But the page was gone, and the boy's name with it. She resigned herself to saying her prayer not for him alone but for all the lost little boys, and for all the lost little girls, which she sometimes believed she was, looking in the mirror, because inside, inside living felt the same, but outside, my God, what happened?

1 DOG, 1 KNIFE

EPISODE 1: "THE MYSTERY OF THE MISSING THING"

IT WAS TERRY'S SECOND TIME TAKING FRESHMAN English, his first with Miss Havergam. She was new: three years out of university and heading classes of her own for the second time. The bad kids rolled in late, if they bothered showing. The okay kids played video games at their desks or flipped through thick decks of Pokémon cards. Mr. Brock, who normally taught English, Shop and Woods, had been put on stress leave after a kid snapped the band saw trying to cut an old laptop in half and Mr. Brock took a swing at him with a two-by-four.

Terry's movies needed to be more current. Miss Havergam told him so.

"Not just current," she added. "Real. Current and *real*."

He typed her every word on his iPad, which the Maplewood High administration had provided him because his handwriting was illegible to his teachers and himself.

Miss Havergam was the only teacher to give him the extra attention the counsellor said he needed to realize his true potential. When they met to chat, she shared some of her lunch with him, squares of Caramilk bar, Hickory Sticks and, on that day, his own napkin piled with Nacho Cheese Doritos. The chips left a pinkish film atop the misspelled words the iPad corrected, changing *finegr* to *finger* and *pols* to *pulse*.

The serialized movies Terry made were not for Miss Havergam's class, but his teacher watched each weekly instalment. He met with her at lunch hour on Wednesdays and she shared her thoughts on the twists that worked and the mysteries that remained too mysterious. He answered questions about his process and intentions, reminding her his action figure actors remained boxed in their packaging because his dad said they would be worth more that way in the years ahead. His movies took place in the near future. That was how he explained away the packaging: protective gear. In this future, the air was lethal.

His mom gave him little gifts to pass along to Miss Havergam to help him show his appreciation: Ghandi quotation–bordered stationery, which Miss Havergam kept on her desk; dried apple chips, which she stuck in her drawer, winking at him, saying, "Treat for later"; a hand-knit scarf, which she wore all winter, bought at a local farmers' market; and organic doggy treats, picked up from the same market for Miss Havergam's rough collie, Buffy – treats Miss Havergam told him to tell his mom "Buffy absolutely hoovered."

Miss Havergam had begun watching Terry's movies at the start of the term, after he announced in class that he ran a YouTube channel, *The Smarthead Files*, where he posted the serialized exploits of his ace detective, Chuck Smarthead, PI. Terry had invited everyone in class to subscribe, though only Miss Havergam, who had written the name of the channel on the board, accepted the invitation. Miss Havergam was supportive like that. She also organized volunteer opportunities for Maplewood students at the humane society and ran the Creative Writing Club at lunch hour on Tuesdays. Terry attended the club for two weeks before he and Miss Havergam saw no one else got *The Smarthead Files*. The one-on-one meetings had been her idea.

At the beginning of each of these meetings, Miss Havergam told Terry he had "quite the imagination," but she also reminded him his type of movies weren't necessarily her cup of tea. Miss Havergam repeated herself often. At least once a week she said she'd been given her dog, Buffy, as a birthday present when she was the same age as Terry's classmates, a year younger than him. Buffy herself was a daily topic, a figure in grammar quizzes and "quick as the wind" when acting as an example in a simile.

Miss Havergam's cup of tea was National Geographic documentaries, *The Voice* and *Dog Whisperer*. Those were all daily topics, too. The girls in class fluttered right into recaps of the singing contest, while the boys groaned. The boys called Miss Havergam "Miss Massive-Cans" behind her back because, as one of the jokers put it, she had knockers the size of oil drums. Another kid bet two dwarves were dozing in hammocks under her blouse. Terry was the only one not to elaborately describe the fluids he longed to shoot on, rub into or lick from Miss Havergam's breasts. Miss Havergam was one of the eight subscribers to his YouTube channel. She had earned the loyalty of his silence.

During that day's lunch hour meeting, when he had finished transcribing Miss Havergam's remarks, Terry puzzled over them briefly and then came right out and asked her what she meant by his movies needing to be more current and real. Miss Havergam said she guessed she meant he needed a bit more of that thing in a movie people connected with, right now, in the moment, that warmed their hearts or, she added with a wink, broke them. He thought about this and then typed. The iPad changed *brake* to *break*.

"But why isn't my work current and real?" he asked.

Miss Havergam gave him a nod he knew meant "good question." She pushed the last few fingers-full of broken Doritos into her mouth and thought.

Terry was buoyed by this nod, as though he had stuck a secret key in a hidden lock and heard the thing click.

She had the answer. His sense of certainty had something to do with the way she wore her hair pulled back too tight in a bun, the way her broad forehead and round cheeks puffed up above her hairline. She smiled at him through her chewing. He smiled at a place above her inflated forehead, so overcome by anticipation he could not return it directly. His fingertips quivered above his iPad's sticky screen.

"Why isn't your work current and real?" Miss Havergam asked herself under her breath.

The chip bag crackled. Her fingers searched its inner-reaches for crumbs.

There was something more to her. There was a deeper, secret being inside her that no one had ever glimpsed. Terry witnessed this in the mask-like swelling of his teacher's face. His eyes lost focus from staring so intently, and it looked as though this woman before him had been scalped, releasing the slick, black, perfect plastic surface of the true self hidden beneath, freeing its skin to glisten in the open air.

"There's just something missing," she finally said, shaking her head.

"What?" Terry coughed, her answer punching the breath right out of him.

"I don't know what else to say, Terry," she added, scrambling. He could tell by the way she sought his attention she knew she had let him down. "There's this thing, and it's not there."

She tilted her head back and quickly dropped the mound of crumbs and flavouring into her mouth. A spot of the bright orange mess remained caked to her chin, below the corner of her lips, after she had anxiously licked her fingers clean.

He wanted his smile to look as real and as current to her as her reassuring smile looked to him. But his disappointment, the queasiness he experienced, trapped by the intense gaze of the Doritos stain, prevented any genuine gratitude from materializing. It stretched his lips into a surgeon's mask – flat and blank.

Terry looked away from the moist, glowing smudge and down at his iPad.

He did not type a word.

The spot of Doritos continued to affect him though, and his deep disappointment transformed into something else. An oddly warm intensity, a swirling like oil and water shaken together in a sealed jar, roiled away in his gut. The flavouring on her face was the same flavouring she had consumed. The same flavouring she had put into herself was the same substance he had taken into his own body. That Doritos dust bound them. He might as well have stood, dove over the desk and licked the spot from her skin with his drying tongue. That act would not have brought them any closer. Their bond, through the chips, was already complete. And this was the bond – their link, the thing – he needed to capture in the next instalment of *The Smarthead Files*. The bell sounded.

Its ringing, he knew, could not break the bodily throbbing that umbilicaled them. He was free to be consumed by their connection everywhere else.

He stood without looking up.

"Thank you, Miss Havergam," he said, and started for the door.

She called him back. "I hope I didn't hurt your feelings, Terry."

"No," he said, seeing with relief she had wiped the Doritos from her chin.

"Here," she said, reaching for her desk drawer. She withdrew a half-eaten Dairy Milk bar and broke him off two squares. Taking them, he glanced down into the drawer's open mouth. There were dozens of plastic bags inside, filled with what looked like shrivelled human ears. They were apple chips, all the uneaten goodies he had given her.

EPISODE 2: "THE SWEET FEEL OF KILLING KILLED"

At his desk in the back corner of his fourth period Biology class, Terry avoided the glare of the blank page of his iPad. He watched Mrs. Pardinas as she explained the process by which plants bent to face the sun. He watched the leaves of the trees outside the window for evidence of this process. He reread the shots fired in the battle taking place between the anonymous students who shared his desk during different periods. His iPad's screen remained void.

The desk fight had started last week. The student whose penmanship reminded Terry of soap bubbles had written, "What do you want?"

"For you to blow me," a student had replied in all caps.

"Me, too," the next student had added in slanted letters.

Terry did not have a pencil or a pen. He could not interrupt the clash and ask, "How can I make my next movie real?" ·

Mrs. Pardinas explained that plants do not exactly "turn." Instead, the cells of the plant nearest the sun shrink, while the cells farthest from the sun grow. An animation in her PowerPoint demonstrated this swelling of the cells in the shadow, the effect of this force. The two most recent remarks in the desk war were, in all caps, "Suck my balls faggot," and, in soap bubble penmanship, "Once your dad teaches me how."

Terry returned to that first question: "What do you want?"

He wanted Miss Havergam.

"Miss Havergam," he typed.

A smoke-soft tingle drifted up from the letters as he typed them. This smouldering travelled through his hand, up his arm to his shoulder, rising from his neck into his ears, which pulsed with sound, as though a winged-thing's egg laid there long ago had finally hatched. Her name contained her. It diminished her to a size he could protect. He wanted his movie to protect her, what he felt for her.

He was a massive glass dome lowering over her city before the great flood came to wipe out the world. Sharks would swim on the other side of the glass as life went on, schools of sea horses, great whales. He licked his fingers and wiped out the war of words the desk had preserved. The great whales of possible movie scenarios – from the basest, ageless murder plots to an epic journey to the centre of the sun – swam in hulking, sense-clouding masses through his brain. He licked his fingers again. He erased everything but the question, the first words.

He never consciously made up his movies.

They played in his mind.

He transcribed.

In that moment, though, none of the films projected inside him met Miss Havergam's criteria. But what could be more current than his experience, dipping his head into the stream and extracting gold? What could be more real?

Each of the serial killers Smarthead had brought to justice had arisen in an effortless flash, from the Silver Screen Killer (who murdered his victims by mimicking the death scenes from Hollywood blockbusters) to the Google Killer (who found his victims using a search algorithm designed to locate the most anti-social individuals) to the Look-Alike Killer (whose victims all resembled C-list celebrities) and on and on and on.

These same visions told him why Tony Stark's moustache and wry grin made him perfect to play the PI. They told him how to compose his packaged toy actors before the filming frame. They told him which voice to use in post-production to bring to life the different *Arkham City*, Chogokin, *The Clone Wars*, *Power Rangers*, Minimate, Minifig, *Transformers* and *Band of Brothers* figures who peopled his world: the serial killers, their victims and the rest of the cops, worried parents, cruel parents, politicians, drug dealers, street people and orphaned children, who either sustained the whole sick system or suffered at its hands.

The birth of Smarthead's catchphrase was another example. Terry had been down in the basement, escaping the roar of the neighbour's lawn mower. Those sorts of loud things, unrelenting, undid him. He had pressed the two pillows tighter to his ears, and then he heard it: "Your days of killing have just been killed." The final episode of each story arc ended with Smarthead delivering this guarantee. The phrase turned a tap in his mind, releasing the sweet feeling of "justice served" into the fist and jaw and spine. It signalled to Terry's current ten to twenty-five viewers to stay tuned next week for a new case. In the future, he was certain, thousands, if not hundreds of thousands of viewers would receive this signal from this same killer line.

By his fifth period Health class, Terry had settled on an idea. Miss Havergam had once mentioned she was half-English and that her grandfather still lived in an English village near the sea. What if she went to visit her grandfather and discovered everyone she knew there, including her grandfather, had vanished? What if the village was in ruins? What if a mysterious corporation had taken possession of the fishery?

The idea to add a corporation came from Mr. Roy. In their first class, he admitted he was being forced to teach Health because of cuts to the Fine Arts budget. As was their daily ritual, Terry's classmates had easily coaxed Mr. Roy off the topic of self-esteem and into one of his rants against banks and corporations.

Terry opened up the browser on his iPad. Following Miss Havergam's advice, he wanted to find the name of a real corporation to serve as his movie's bad guy, preferably a company currently guilty of the sins Mr. Roy condemned. Instead, he found the real subject for the film he would make for her. The top headline on the *Star*'s website read, "Luka Rocco Magnotta Sought as Body Parts Case Turns into Horror Show."

It felt like a current. Was that why she had used that word? The real facts swept him away in a surge: the brutal murder; the murderer's brutal propagation of his poor victim, through the mail and the video "1 Lunatic, 1 Ice Pick"; the murderer's surgically modified face; his lifelong quest for fame; his ever-changing appearance; his failed reality TV stardom; the fact that the owner of Bestgore. com kept the snuff film posted because "people had the right to see the truth, reality without censorship"; the fact that the killer was still on the loose; the fact that the killer could kill again.

What if Magnotta killed again?

A scenario struck Terry, projecting from the ether beyond the iPad screen onto the screen in his mind. From this vision, he transcribed his script. He remained in his desk after class until the custodian kicked him out. He typed on the bus, at the dinner table, so enraptured his mom had to remind him to take his pills. Switching from his iPad to his MacBook after dinner, he continued beside his parents who made him watch a televised spelling bee with them, on the edge of the tub while he pretended to bathe, and at his packaged-action-figure-cluttered desk. When he crawled into bed at 3:30 a.m., his script was finished. He faked sick the next morning, and then filmed, edited and mixed sound all day and into the night. An hour after his mom kissed him good night, he finished "Episode 1: The Message Inside the Murder," the first instalment of *The Case of the Custom-Made Killer*.

"Episode 1" was composed of four scenes. In the first scene, Chuck Smarthead, PI, receives a taunting phone call from Luka Magnotta. Magnotta promises he will kill again and suggests he has hidden clues to his next victim's identity in the video of his first crime. The second scene takes place in Miss Havergam's classroom. Miss Havergam, played by the *Arkham City* Catwoman, and Terry, played by a Minimate Batman, discuss with excitement their upcoming class trip to the zoo. Smarthead scours Magnotta's gruesome video for clues in scene three; his search is fruitless. In the fourth and final scene, Magnotta enters his hideout. He is played by one of *The Clone Wars* clones, though he does not retain this form for long. He enters his Instant Plastic Surgery Machine and exits as Terry, the Minimate Batman, a tinfoil knife taped to his packaging. Magnotta, in his new guise, hisses, "Enjoy the zoo, Miss Havergam, because this visit will be your last!" The episode ends with his twisted cackle.

Terry, as was his ritual, watched the episode as soon as it was uploaded, giving the piece its first official YouTube view. It gave him chills. The cliffhanger left even him wanting to see what was going to happen next. And having watched the video on the web, in the world, coming to him from out there, he was more impressed by his inspired decision to include an actual clip from Magnotta's "1 Lunatic, 1 Ice Pick" as Smarthead searches the sick artifact for clues. In the clip, the victim, bound, is straddled. That's it. No visible violence. The horror is in knowing what is to come.

Normally, Terry would have waited for Miss Havergam to find the first instalment on her own. For this one, though, he could not wait. He sent her an email with the subject line "One Thousand Scarves for You (and a Thousand Treats for Buffy)." He sincerely thanked her for her wisdom. The reward promised in the subject line would not cover his debt; he hoped the latest instalment of *The Smarthead Files* could.

He wanted to witness her view registering, but the count remained at one no matter how many times he hit Refresh. She might have been in bed already. She lived on the second floor of a surprisingly rundown four-storey apartment building. If she was asleep, he could throw rocks at her balcony window and wake her and tell her to watch. It was an hour-and-a-half walk from his place, though it might have been shorter. The one time he had done it he had trudged through a foot of snow. Back when they were first getting to know one another, he had tracked down her address in a PDF on the humane society website.

Exhausted by a full day of work, and running on a few hours of sleep, he barely had the energy to keep refreshing his browser. He slouched in his chair and watched his email inbox for the arrival of her thankful reply. None of the numbers he wanted to change changed. His head lolled away from his MacBook's glow.

EPISODE 3: "THE CASE OF THE CLIFFHANGER THAT WOULD NEVER END"

Terry arrived at school early. There could be no delays. He needed to ask Miss Havergam, as soon as he could, "What do you think of what I made for you?"

The class was empty. He took his seat in the back, not wanting to appear too eager by waiting at her desk. Two girls from the Creative Writing Club arrived first. One of them flipped on the classroom lights, while the other made a comment about how creepy it was to sit alone in the dark. He glanced up from his iPad with each new arrival. The video had a total of three views. One of the viewers had to have been Miss Havergam, but her usual view-signalling Like was absent. The Like button could not contain what she was feeling.

He watched the door intently, waiting for this feeling and its lovely bearer to enter the room. The bell rang. A balding man with a light bulb–shaped dome slid into the class with a celebratory, "Made it." He wore a blue velvet jacket and one of those pointy, well-trimmed chin beards Terry associated with science-prone supervillains. Before the man could say a word, Terry exclaimed over the class's quieting din, "You're not Miss Havergam."

"That's right," the man grinned, eyeing up Terry. "I'm your substitute teacher, Mr. Weiss. You must be the sharp one."

The class erupted. No one but Terry asked where Miss Havergam was. His question went unanswered.

"Since you're so sharp," Mr. Weiss said, "I bet you can help me find someone I'm looking for." Mr. Weiss glanced down at the paper in his hand and read Terry's name.

"That's me," Terry said.

"Should have guessed. The principal wants to talk to you, pronto."

He wished for a cliffhanger. He wished for a week to pass between the moment he rose from his desk and the moment he reached the threshold of the door. He slumped weakly through the hall, nauseated, wishing his life was one of those shows where the fans voted for who lived and who loved in next week's instalment. He wished he could cast the deciding vote. He had no idea what awaited him in Principal Drummel's office. Worse, he could not help but imagine the impossible: Miss Havergam waiting in the principal's place, her fingers blouse-button-perched, eager to set free all her pain-erasing flesh.

The secretary pulled the door closed behind him.

"I want you to know right off the bat, mister," Principal Drummel said, "that if it was entirely up to me, I would expel you."

Terry dropped into the seat by the door, unable to make it to the chair Principal Drummel pointed to in front of her desk. He felt his mouth dangle open, convulse, like he was coughing up an eel. His initial suspension would last a week. Principal Drummel glared down at him as she advanced.

Words finally formed: "What did I do?"

"What did you do? You made that sick threat against your teacher and your school."

"What?"

"Your movie!"

A deep sense of relief spilled through him. Principal Drummel went on about this type of intimidation not being tolerated, and the necessity of police involvement. He barely heard a word. It had all been a misunderstanding. There were hands that could reach from the shore and rescue him from the current that threatened to sweep him away.

Did Miss Havergam know what was happening to him? She was more than likely sick at home with the flu, curled up in bed with Buffy and her laptop. She was re-watching his movie. With the whole day ahead of her, she would re-enjoy his life's work. Buffy would nuzzle closer for a scratch, and scratching her life-long companion Miss Havergam would sigh, "I wish Terry was with us." She was seconds from sending him an email: "I wish you were here."

"I need to talk to Miss Havergam," Terry said.

"You have no right to talk to her."

"But she can explain the movie. It was her idea."

Principal Drummel swallowed whatever she was about to say. Her looming face tightened with puzzlement.

"Terry," she said, "Miss Havergam is the one who reported you."

It returned.

The current.

The hands meant to save him from drowning revealed themselves to be the watery force. Miss Havergam dragged him under. She was as endless as violent waters. In her deception, his betrayer was endless. It did not take a Chuck Smarthead to see her fingerprints all over his punishments. She was his punisher, his puppeteer. He was a packaged-action figure in her beefy paws. How many others had she seduced to control?

Miss Havergam, disguised as Principal Drummel, took away his iPad. If the police found grounds for a criminal complaint, she promised, he would be expelled. If no charges were laid, she would force him to transfer to an institution better able to handle him.

Miss Havergam, speaking through the zombified minds of his parents, took away his MacBook, iPod, Xbox, PSP, microphone and camera. His future internet use, if the courts did not ban him for good, would be strictly monitored.

"No more YouTube, ever," Miss Havergam spit through his mind-controlled dad. "And that channel of yours is gonzo."

He stood to protest in the name of his subscribers, to object to the erasure of the views he had worked so hard to earn. His Miss Havergam-ed dad, who would normally not lay a fingertip on him, pushed him with both hands so hard his chair tipped away from the kitchen table. His mom wept. Miss Havergam allowed her tears, but nothing more. He bawled on the floor and his mom did not move to hold him tight.

His dad, red-faced, barked question after question:

"What did you think would happen if you threatened to kill your teacher?"

"What if this maniac had seen your video and came here to hurt me and your mom?"

"What are this murdered kid's parents supposed to feel when they hear you were making light of their son's death?"

His dad sent him to his room to think about these questions. But he did not think about any of them. The question he wanted to ask was: Why?

That question, to begin, was a syllable. It was a sound to make – as good as any other – when he bawled. His pillow muffled it, made it senseless. The meal he picked at in bed barely interrupted its sputtering. His mom silenced its verbalization as she stoked his back and said, "Hush now," and he pretended to fall asleep.

In those hours of sleeplessness, something so simple and yet so profound dawned on him. He had invented Chuck Smarthead, PI. This fact wiped all of the despair and self-pity off that "why" and made it an actual question. It was a question he, the real Chuck Smarthead, could answer.

Why did she do it? Like every good PI knew, to answer that question he first had to ask: How? At his desk, he wrote out his theories in a notebook half-filled with math homework. He tested those theories on page after page, distilled the facts and compiled them. Everyone was involved: the Creative Writing Club, Principal Drummel, the Maplewood High administration, YouTube. More: his viewers, his non-viewers (them especially), his parents, the Maplewood High custodians, the sub, Mr. Brock, the kid who had cut the laptop in half and gotten Mr. Brock fired.

His writing was so messy that the notes he had written at 1:00 a.m. were unreadable by 3:00. The 4:00 a.m. epiphany – underlined, starred and circled – was, by 7:00, nothing more than a hammer-smashed hieroglyphic. His writing resembled strands of knotted spiderweb, a fact he found so perfect because what he had revealed in his words was the pattern of the web in which he was ensnared. His mom brought him breakfast, which he pretended to eat to get rid of her, and then he mapped out the web, writing down the name of each body his betrayer had wielded against him and drawing the line that connected each body back to her. Really, they were each as much of a mosquito as he was. They had not stirred enough to realize they had been caught in her web.

He knew the answer. Why bring all of these forces together and wield them against him? Because he could make what she never could. She had seen his serials before coming to Maplewood, marvelled at how masterfully he worked with the form. She had arranged the job opportunity so she could earn his trust, encourage this and advise against that, until he made the perfect cliffhanger. And he had finally done it, and she had ruined him.

She had downloaded the movie before shutting down his YouTube channel. She had posted it on her own channel. It was already going viral under her name. But she was not doing it for the fame. There was something more sinister at work. He could feel it. By silencing him, she had set something monstrous free in the world: the cliffhanger that would never end. The world would screech to a halt as the cliffhanger spread via shares and retweets and old-fashioned word-of-mouth recommendations. Its endlessness would lead to endless re-watching, endless speculation on what would come next, endless inattention to all the basic world-sustaining tasks.

The world was going to end.

He needed to save it.

He needed to finish *The Case of the Custom-Made Killer*.

The script would have to be entirely rewritten. With the mix of rage and fear he felt at Miss Havergam's horrific plan propelling him, he saw the crime that perfectly expressed the breadth and depth of her evil. His lack of sleep and, as he wrote the day away, his lack of sustenance from the lunch and dinner he barely touched, aided him, intensifying his vision.

The movie begins with Magnotta dying after exiting his Instant Plastic Surgery Machine, and Miss Havergam leaving Maplewood to return to her position as CEO of the Havergam Corporation. Meanwhile, somewhere in Africa, a young man returns home after four years at university to find his family, friends and neighbours have all vanished. The empty village is an unrecognizable ruin and the Havergam Corporation now owns the village's oil wells. The young man hires Smarthead to solve the case.

After some top-notch sleuthing and escaping multiple attempts on his life by Miss Havergam's serial killer henchmen, Smarthead discovers the horrible truth. Miss Havergam had invented the twenty-first century's first true horror, which she gives different names in different scenes: ethical colonialism, ethical genocide, ethical ethnic cleansing. A dome that sped up the passing of generations, named the E-Geno Dome, had been placed over the village. Inside the E-Geno Dome, the people were well provided for, autonomously ruled themselves and experienced time passing at a normal pace. In truth, though, one E-Geno Dome century was relative to one real world hour.

"In less than a day," Miss Havergam enthusiastically explains to a cuffed and bound Smarthead, "the domed society spends generations adapting, centuries flourishing and dies off in its own natural way."

Later, in the serial's final scene, Miss Havergam dangles from a rope above a hole in one of her E-Geno Domes. Smarthead pilots his chopper with one arm and holds the rope with the other.

"But I am good," Miss Havergam half-pants and half-screams, desperate for Smarthead's mercy. "Everyone wins. We gain access to resources the world desperately needs. The people receive real-time reparations. And the lifespan of their society runs its natural –"

The rope snaps under Miss Havergam's weight and she disappears into the E-Geno Dome.

"Your days of killing," Smarthead smirks, piloting his chopper against the backdrop of the setting sun, "have just been killed."

EPISODE 4: "THE BLOODY KNIFE"

The ladder was perfect. Another surge of strengthening joy rushed from his gut to his limbs as the rubber-covered top of the aluminum ladder found stucco and another piece of his plan snapped perfectly into place. The ladder reached four feet above the metal rail of Miss Havergam's balcony. Stepping from the ladder to her balcony to the inside of her apartment would be a breeze.

Thinking ahead to his entry into her apartment, he pulled off his shoes and socks. Quiet, as he knew from working on

Smarthead, would be key. He judged the weight of the camera bag slung around his shoulder and then struggled up the ladder. Everything he needed was in the bag: the camera, a flashlight, zaleplon-stuffed sausage chunks, a butcher knife, garbage bags, duct tape, a pocket pry bar and a hammer.

This feeling of fortifying joy had been his companion as he snuck through the night to Miss Havergam's, the joyous surge a low hum each second he remained unseen and then bursting when he found the perfect ladder sticking out of the grass beside a back alley garage. He drew a similar ecstatic strength from Miss Havergam's cherished pet, Buffy. He was there for her. The excellence of his casting of his new script made him feel the way God must have felt casting that first sun from light and, admiring its glory, musing, yes, more.

Buffy was to be one of the stars of his rewrite of *The Case of the Custom-Made Killer*. He knew a good spot in River Park. The clearing would not make an ideal Africa, but it would offer him lots of cover and the park resided halfway between Miss Havergam's apartment and his home. He had decided to cast Buffy as all of the villagers wiped out by the Havergam Corporation's selfish ends. A garbage bag would play the E-Geno Dome. The only camera he could find did not shoot video, but it would have to do. It was his dad's old point-and-shoot digital, a long-term resident of the abandoned electronics drawer in the entertainment room.

His plan had been to step onto the balcony's concrete lip then swing his leg over the rail like a sheriff swinging his leg over his stallion. The rail, though, was too high, so he climbed up another two rungs. His mind geysered visions of what he was going to make. He stepped his bare left foot onto the balcony's top rail. If he caused Miss Havergam one one-thousandth of the pain she had inflicted on him, he would be satisfied. The railing gave under his weight. It swung in as the loose bolts pulled right out of the stucco. One confused thought caught him: balconies don't work like this.

He pushed away from the fall, aiming to find his balance again on the ladder, but he pushed too hard. The ladder tipped. He went down with it.

Something returned – a small point of visibility and sound. A light came on in the window of the ground-floor apartment above him. The curtains did not move. The light went out. He was on his back in the grass. It was night. He sensed more, but the more his senses returned, the less he could see. The pain overtook his experience. His forehead throbbed like a squirrel had crawled inside to feed. His right foot was a blazing mess. A stilled meteor had merged with it. His pinkie toe had snapped back. It dangled from a shred of skin. He vomited at the sensation and the sight.

When he tried to sit up, his stomach screamed and his hand reached for the agony, palmed blood-soaked hoodie. Tearing off his hoodie, he found more blood, more pain. Ripping off his T-shirt, he discovered it: the hole. It was in his left side. It was the size of the mouth of a life-sized baby doll, opening. It ran in a neat vertical line below his rib cage. He reached for his camera bag. The butcher knife had sliced through the leather when he had hit the ground. By the blood on the blade, he guessed the thing had driven three inches into him. He hoped not. The wound drooled more blood.

He cried, but he refused to let himself cry out for help. He whispered the word in the sobs he muted as best as he could: help help help help help. He did not want Miss Havergam to see this. He did not want her to hear him cry out in defeat. She would have left him there anyway, even if he had called to her, even if he had begged, Please, let's take it all back. That thought made him cry harder, tears of rage mixing with tears of sadness and pain. She would have stepped out on the balcony and spit something cruel about how stupid he was for not having tested the railing before stepping on it, or she would have glanced down at him like he was a turd in a toilet bowl before flushing him from sight.

He did not want her to see what he did to deal with his mangled foot. He did not want her to witness him dressing his wounds with a combination of duct tape and shreds of his hoodie. He did not want her to behold him nearly faint when he stood, catch himself, then make the climb, his efforts eased by the busted rail, and crouch before her sliding balcony door. He wanted her to have to guess, to have to test the limits of her imagination to grasp what he was capable of when she woke in the morning and her dog was gone and she found in its place a bloody, mangled toe.

EPISODE 5: "THE RETURN OF THE MYSTERY OF THE MISSING THING"

He peered into her apartment through the sliding door. His injured foot could handle zero pressure, so he sat with his right leg extended. He was surprised by the sparseness of her things. Only the entertainment stand, filled with a widescreen TV and packed with DVDs, matched his vision of her world. He had anticipated heaps of furniture and masses of blankets and loads of framed pictures filling every free inch. Three rectangles dotted the bare walls. The one half-visible in the light of a distant street lamp was a photograph of Buffy. There was no other sign of his star.

He worked the pry bar under the sliding door. He had learned this trick on the internet in the winter when he had thought of leaving Miss Havergam a surprise bouquet. He covered the exposed end of the pry bar with a bundle of T-shirt to mute the sound of the hammer. He waited for Buffy's growling face to appear at the window, or Miss Havergam's face transitioning from sleepy annoyance to incited shock, or the faces of the officers who would put him away forever. His head throbbed with an oddly seductive pain, a hand passing gently over his eyes to summon sleep. Each time he tapped the pry bar too hard, the stab torched his side, jolting him back to attention. The window remained free of faces except his own determined reflection.

Once the pry bar was snug under the door, he gave it a hard clockwise turn with both hands. The lock popped out. His hand shot into his bag, and with a wince he slid the door open and tossed in a handful of pill-stuffed sausage bits. He counted on their aroma catching Buffy's attention before she spotted him and barked so wildly she woke the whole building. He retrieved the butcher knife, just in case.

He waited. The blood overwhelmed his bandages. He scratched the knife gently across the glass, hoping to draw the dog out. When his foot spasmed in pain, it squished inside his shoe, like he had emerged from a flooded basement. The waistband of his jeans soaked up the blood leaking from his side. He tapped the glass. Buffy did not show.

He slid the door open. He left everything on the balcony but the knife. The pain in his foot was worsening so he had to crawl in on all fours. He had not imagined entering like that, or being hit with the thick, sour odour of boiled turnips, or hearing Miss Havergam snoring out a cranky snarl in her bedroom.

He caught his breath at the coffee table. He sprawled across it, his need for a recharge outweighing his worry about leaving blood. He listened closely to Miss Havergam's snoring and thought he heard Buffy's snore whining underneath it, a tin whistle accompanying a motorcycle engine. Both sounds might have been Miss Havergam. He hoped so. If Buffy was asleep with her in bed, he was not sure what he would do, what he might have to do. He leaned forward to retrieve one of his sausage bits from the rug.

He froze.

Buffy sat at attention at the entrance of the hallway. He could make out her silhouette as his eyes adjusted to the dark. She stared at him intently from beside the entertainment stand. He remained leaned forward, clutching the sausage, though his nerves raged and his shoulder quivered, growing weak. He had not heard her approach. As his vision adjusted, he could see the bedroom door was closed. Buffy had most likely been curled up there. After all Miss Havergam's talk of love and loyalty and companionship, he was surprised she would not share a bed with her best friend.

On the verge of collapsing, he braced his right side against the coffee table and lifted the treat off the rug. Buffy did not flinch.

He judged the distance and tossed the sleep-inducing treat. Right away he could tell he had overshot the mark. In anticipation of her attack, his right hand tightened on the knife, and a second surge of energy diminished the chorus of his injuries, diminished his body's incessant request to sleep.

The treat struck Buffy's nose and dropped to the carpet. Buffy did not budge. Cautiously, he lowered his body to the floor, and when she still remained at attention he crawled to her as fast as he could. He released the knife to speed his approach and allow him, as he rose to his knees to meet her gaze, to grab her with both hands.

Buffy was already dead. She was not completely dead. She was stuffed, alive in appearance. There was no heat to her body, but there was life to her lush pelt, in the solidity of the tooth that poked his cheek as he reached to brush her bushy tail. He sensed this life as he stroked her in disbelief, holding back the laughter that threatened to erupt in a full, carefree, barking flourish. Buffy smiled, ready to laugh with him.

The moment was alive with possibility. He could carry her to the woods, as planned, and film the opening scene for his movie. He could break into Maplewood and leave Buffy on Miss Havergam's desk for her students to see the real state of her oldest friend. He could give Buffy to his parents and Principal Drummel as Exhibit A in his case against his accuser. She was not fit to judge him. He could head straight into her bedroom with Buffy in tow and prove to her she was not fit to accuse him, to teach him, to own his love.

Whichever possibility he chose, he would have to pick Buffy up. He tried, hugging her, embracing her under the gut and muzzle. Every inch of his body begged him to leave his head buried in her soft fur, to take a quick nap to recover, but he willed his hands to keep searching for an adequate hold. Then the thought hit him: this would make a great cliffhanger. Once Smarthead went global, and all the major producers finished bidding over the rights to his life story, this moment would make a perfect ending to episode number one, or to the first movie. Everyone in the audience would need to know: What would happen next?

He wondered how he looked, grabbing Buffy in this way and that. He stopped searching for a hold, needing to wait for the pain in his side to subside, and he thought about this, leaning his full weight into her fur. He shut his eyes. He tried to see himself from the point of view of a lens set up on the threshold of the balcony's open door, from the perspective of the director's chair he would occupy in the decades ahead.

How would he describe it to the actor? Move like a police officer checking for weapons. Move like a doctor searching for a pulse, searching a whole body for deadly growths or signs of life. He would tell the kid playing him to try it all as they rehearsed before shooting. Do it like you are exhausted in the night and hunting for your lover's ear, even if you do not speak your lover's language. Do it like you are probing for the mouth of an alien life you are certain is about to starve, even if you do not know the creature's poison from its food. It did not matter. What mattered was that one day he would finally get to say what he had never said when making movies in his room, or, truth be told, what he did whisper sometimes to launch a scene, faking the snap of the clapperboard with his hands, even though there was no one outside of himself to hear his words: action, okay now, go.

THE POEM

THE POEM BEGAN AFTER THE WAITER SAID, "Binoculars are against the law." *Indecent* was the word the waiter struggled for and the poet helped him find. This was in Morocco in 1989, on the first trip the poet took after leaving home at the age of nineteen. Inside her, this autonomic system of synapse and sensibility inhaled a big breath of world and right away she saw the town from the restaurant terrace resembled a crowd of bowed men. It *was* indecent, those invasions the curved lenses permitted, the intimacy they invented between eye and rooftop, eye and half-curtained window, eye and the line where the flaking, sun-worn crown of the minaret swelled like a fine, aged breast, like a breath-puffed cheek, like a mittened fist into the most exquisite and elemental sky. She hid the binoculars out of view on her lap under the table.

"No, no," the waiter apologized, "you're not in trouble."

He gestured for her to return the binoculars to her eyes and explore the afternoon. "It's wrong for locals. For us."

That was the Poem: the way the waiter tapped his chest when he said, "For us"; the way, at first, he wouldn't look at the binoculars when she asked if he wanted to try. The waiter finally relented. He accepted them uncertainly with both hands. Judging from his backward glances at the empty tables, ghosts she could not see possessed those chairs, commanding "no" in the wails of the one God's newborns, voices that were the bursting mists where the ocean of law struck shore.

The waiter transformed into the wagtails, the falcon, the menagerie of birds he tracked with the binoculars and pointed out to her. The poet's eyes welled up. The depth of her skin grew palpable along her arms and neck and back. The sensation made her feel like she was filling with a colony of summer-heated ants. Somewhere inside her a home was exposed; it longed to house forever the way the waiter flapped and fluttered and dove from the north edge of the terrace to the east to the south and back to the north, the way he left to seek different heights and flocks, returning in five-minute intervals, sometimes with portions of her meal, to share news of this specific distance collapsed and this specific, simple want amplifying as it neared what it wanted.

"I wish my wife was here," the waiter said more than once, the last being after he returned the binoculars and brought the bill. Each time he said it, his eyes widened, as though he had been struck by the name of the thief in a heist flick, by the missing variable of a formula he'd wrestled for years, by the weight of missing years certain amnesiacs must feel while peeling page by page through piles of old photo albums and old diaries and old correspondence from strangers whose status as acquaintance or true friend remains as indeterminate and indefinable as your own reflected face would be if you spent a lifetime staring at the sun.

* * *

The Poem barely survived the trip back to Canada. For months, it remained an assembly of notes and unfinished drafts in the poet's notebook. It was the poet's first time in Toronto, and her transition to the new city was hardly eased by the artist couple that had swarmed her in Spain, buzzing, "You *must* move to Toronto" and promising her a couch and a job. She had met them backpacking on her way to the Basque region, where she had heard you could make money picking on farms, though picking *what* she had not been sure. The artists had been undertaking research for a performance piece on matadors but had called it quits early to strike out for Germany. They wanted to grab a few particles of the freedom swirling in the ruins of the newly fallen Berlin Wall.

The job in Toronto turned out to be a volunteer position (due to a failed grant application) at the gallery the artists ran. They charged their fellow creators to display their creations. "Just as you can't put a price on work experience," ran the party line, "you can't put a price on experienced work." The couch was back-breakingly trendy, clean-lined and spotless yet robust with a funk suggestive of mushrooms picked fresh from deep, deep woods. The poet's plan for her trip had specifically been *not* to plan her return. On the flight out of Vancouver International six months earlier, she wrote a poem with a line that summed up her initiative: "seek to be among things as they stand." At night she woke on the couch evacuated of the will to scribble in the dark anything more than "What now?"

Eventually, she saved enough money working as a nude model to rent a room, and she translated the valuable experience she gained volunteering at the gallery into a job serving coffee. Yet despite the expanding of the time she had to write from minutes to hours, the poet's attempts to fully form the Poem remained unsuccessful. It was not a question of beginning. On its own volition the memory of that moment in Morocco would overtake her without warning – as she reached for the exact Boston cream doughnut a customer requested, as she rode a people-packed streetcar to her GED class – and she would be overcome by the buzzing up and down her arms of a hive of candle-bearing bees.

But none of the versions of the Poem she wrote, enrapt in these flashes, felt complete.

The editors at the literary journals she submitted the Poem to confirmed this feeling. Other poems from her trip were accepted for publication: the Eiffel Tower villanelle, the Amsterdam aubade, the confessional lyric about what happened in the taxi in Glasgow. All the Poem ever received were form rejections, the best of them personalized with vague, conflicting critical blips like "too blindly colonialist" or "too overtly political." Sometimes, as she struggled to revise the Poem, she felt like a first responder lowering into the far-bottomed crevasse the Poem had tumbled into. Other times, she was the one who had plunged into the pit and she waited and waited for rescue, until the Poem finally called down with the news that she could not be saved.

Two years later, the Poem was all but abandoned. The poet's first book, *The Young Woman's Guide to the End of the World*, was heading to final proofs and the Poem did not survive the last round of revisions. The decision to cut the Poem was made mutually. The editor still found it "too tell-y," particularly the bit about the binoculars "transforming vision." The poet couldn't shake the feeling the Poem was missing something crucial, like it was a globular blob of organs, flesh and brains, lacking any sign of a fibula, thumb bone or skull.

Exhausted by the search for the Poem's skeleton, the poet cultivated any distraction to escape the impulse to revise. She typed up the notes from last semester's courses. She perpetually reorganized her bookshelf by the colour of the spine, by national origin, by theme, by length and then back to the spine's colour again. During her lunch break at the U of T Bookstore, she went so far as to play her first video game. The co-worker who owned the Game Boy showed her how to fit the falling blocks into place to stop the pile from accumulating and choking the throat of the screen. She was as enchanted as she was disgusted. This, in the flickering of the millennium's last decade, was the pinnacle of technology? Shrink the factory to something palm-sized. Make the meaningless task the self-absorbing end. Make self-absorption so incredibly and ecstatically mobile.

"You can keep it," her co-worker said, breaking her from the grey pixel trance as he pulled on his jacket.

"What's that?" she asked.

"I'm cutting out early to finish an essay," he said. "You can give the Game Boy back to me tomorrow."

The poet pushed the game into her co-worker's hands and hurried to the counter for a pen. That was what the Poem was missing, the "keep it" – the obvious offer she had failed to make to the waiter. She had failed not out of selfishness, but distraction. So wrapped up in hanging onto the images and impressions that would become the Poem, she had accepted the binoculars from the waiter without thinking to say, "They're yours." That was the Poem: this failure. Back at her apartment, she plucked the heat-defeating birds from this draft, the palpable Plasticine sky from another, her nerves gone mad like moths in light. By morning, it was done. The Poem, read over the phone to her editor, was met by approval and advice about where it should appear in the manu-script. Buoyed by this good news, the poet visited the office of the arts editor of the student newspaper before class. The arts editor had asked for some work and, reading the Poem, she agreed it was perfect for The Poet's Corner, the poetry section of *The Varsity*. She promised to publish it by the end of the month.

On page 76 of *The Young Woman's Guide to the End of the World* and page 19 of *The Varsity*, the Poem, complete, entered the world. By the length of its lines, its steady patience in ink, the affable interaction of its infinite internal shapes with the "will be," "was" and "is" of our saintly, sailing selves, the Poem expressed the manacle-smacking desire to free stuff from its silence, its imper-manence, its pseudo-salves and mock healings, all the et ceteras of the sources of impossible vision. It wanted to be the 12-step program to beauty, the thief who snuck truth into the pockets of the masses mobbed by the miserly vitality of ignorance and the inane. The Poem wanted to un-break us. It wanted to be the crazy cowboy who rode us in reverse and made us wild.

But none of the Poem's longings came to pass. In their place, one Level II ESL student found the Poem in *The Varsity* and memorized it for a recitation assignment. She received a 9.5 out of 10 after nailing it, her slips being the *the* she changed to an *an* and her pronunciation of *reed* as *red*. The book publisher's father was reminded of his trip to Marrakesh after skimming the Poem and asked his wife if she still had the recipe for that stew with the dates. Meanwhile, the piece on the page opposite the Poem, about crossing the Mediterranean Sea in a doorless helicopter, received praise for its "thrilling ingenuity" in the book's first and only review. The piece eight pages before the Poem became the most read poem in the book because of where the spine naturally flipped open. Fifty-four pages before and sixteen pages after the Poem, respectively, were printed the two poems that would soon be anthologized in *Never Never North: New Canadian Poetry*. Nothing of note happened to – or because of – the Poem for years, even after *The Young Woman's Guide to the End of the World* was republished a decade later (along with the poet's second book, *Good Time Kimchi*), the poet having received a major national award for her third collection, *One Who Is Born Under the Sign of Cancer*, a poetic history of figures for the moon.

* * *

In September 2005, at the start of the Poet's second year teaching creative writing courses at the University of New Brunswick, she had a dream about the waiter. In her dream, the waiter woke her in a stone room without windows. She struggled groggily under blankets on the floor as he shook the lid of a Tim Hortons coffee cup in front of her face while pleading, "Wake up, wake up, wake up." He begged her to show him how to use the lid. To prove it wasn't working, he stood, faced the windowless wall and raised the plastic lid to his eyes with both hands, as though it were a pair of binoculars. He wept and muttered under his breath, "I wanted to show my wife." He moved from wall to wall to wall, trying to see through the lid.

"That's not how it works," the poet said in her dream.

The waiter turned to her. "Then show my wife."

She woke on the floor beside her bed and reached up from the blankets for her pen.

In her office, after discussing prose poetry with her 9:00 a.m. creative writing workshop, she pulled a copy of *The Young Woman's Guide to the End of the World* off her shelf and flipped to the Poem. She needed the table of contents to find it. Repelled by the naïveté of what she had written fifteen years ago, she did not make it past the second stanza. This inspired a bit about not being able to read the Poem, which she added to the poem she had written about her dream. In the ensuing weeks, she added more to this new piece: a section speculating on the whereabouts of the waiter and his wife, a bit about their country's colonial history, lines about her memory of the minarets, her memory of the wagtails, a stanza about the binoculars, another about advances in ocular amplification and another about buying binoculars on eBay, the same make as the pair she had lost long ago. She received a Canada Council grant for the project, with the working title "Lighthouse," and she used the money to return to Morocco. The restaurant was shut down, the building having been converted to a private residence, though no one answered the door any of the times she visited. She could see the terrace of the old restaurant from the rooftop of a different restaurant three blocks east. No one said her binoculars were illegal. No one became a bird. No one wished for a wife. There was no way to find the waiter. She left the binoculars in front of the locked entrance of the former restaurant. The new, book-length poem was published under the title *The Beacon* to rave reviews.

Two lines from *The Beacon*, an oft-underlined passage that figured the nomadity of wounds through desert sands, ended up being employed as the epigraph for *Heal*, a dark satirical novel about the war in Afghanistan. The novelist who wrote it had personally asked the poet's permission to use the quote. In *Heal*, military scientists manipulate a stem cell–born salve developed to restore the skin of burn victims. The new creation, also adminis- tered via a topical solution, renders wounds sentient entities that, hacked from their bodily abodes, relentlessly seek out new bodies upon which to attach themselves in order to be sustained. The protagonist is the scientist who developed the procedure to save burn victims (his brother having committed suicide after being disfigured by an IED outside Kabul) and the story follows his attempt to stop the military when he learns their top-secret plot to deploy the monstrously modified solution. His attempt fails. In the Afghan theatre, he and a platoon of Canadian soldiers are bound and inflicted with ten, fifteen, twenty wounds apiece with bullets, blades, batons and flames. As the scientist and soldiers die, their wounds are brought to life with the topical solution, excised from their bodies and set free in the mountains at the mouth of a Taliban-occupied cave. Impervious to attack, the animated wounds hunt down the insurgents and make their homes on the limbs and chests and heads of the terrorists. The cell is wiped out. The mission is repeated. The war is won.

Heal was an international bestseller. It was optioned for a film, though Paramount would end up rejecting all the novelist's screen- plays. They wanted the climax to celebrate the now-American sol- diers both surviving *and* winning the war. To thank the poet for the epigraph, the novelist nominated her for a mid-career achieve- ment award given biannually at the University of British Columbia, where the novelist taught. The poet won the award and was invited to read. The Poem was also rewarded at the last minute after the poet had made the cross-country trip, her first visit to BC since leaving home nearly two decades earlier. Before the reading, over sushi with the novelist, his fellow faculty members and his top students, one disturbingly cheerful young writer admitted to being "über-inspired" by the poet's early work, and, if it was request hour, he wondered if the poet would read the Poem, which happened to be the beaming student's "total fave." The poet agreed, and later that night, as she took the stage and stepped up to the microphone in the half-filled auditorium, she opened the book to the Poem, which she had never shared at a public reading. The title came out right, just as she had practised it whispering in the bathroom stall of the sushi restaurant, and, before transporting the audience back to that terrace in Morocco, she raised her head to undertake one last exchange of eye contact with her listeners.

She stopped.

Something at the back of the room, something very familiar yet very distant caught her eye, and she squinted slightly to see, to see if it was who she thought it was. The audience followed her gaze to the older woman who had stepped forward from the back wall, her face cast down at her own hands as they fidgeted with the front of a purple, pink and blue wool sweater, far too thick for the weather.

Instead of reading the first line of the Poem, the poet asked into the microphone, "What are you doing here?"

The woman finally looked up from her sweater. "He's dead," she replied.

"Dad?" the poet asked.

The woman, still fidgeting, nodded.

The poet climbed down off the front of the stage and dropped into a crouch. She closed the book and set it beside her on the floor.

"I came here to tell you," the woman added.

The poet stared at the woman, holding back any intervening action with a look that promised she was about to speak. But she didn't speak. Instead, she rose, dusted her legs off and exited through the door at the front of the auditorium, leaving her book on the ground and, on the seat in the front row, her backpack, the copy of *Heal* she had gotten signed for her neighbour and the spring jacket she always wore, regardless of the season.

News of the encounter proliferated quickly. The eyewitness and second-hand accounts – spreading through posts, text messages, emails and phone calls – were supplemented by four photos and a twenty-second video of the poet crouched on the ground.

In the video, the poet seemed to make a strange hum, but, as one YouTube commenter noted, the sound was the buzzing of the auditorium's overhead lights. The event was strange enough, and the poet famous enough, for the *Vancouver Courier* to assign a reporter to find and interview the woman in the sweater. Every lead was a dead end, and the reporter was forced to write about the rumours on the newspaper's blog. The most popular cast the woman as the poet's mother. The father had always been sickly, thus putting the burden of running the family farm, orchard or business on the mother and children. The poet, as a budding artist, had needed to escape this life of hard labour. Another rumour pitched the woman as the poet's older sister, proposing the father had abused them both. The poet was racked with guilt for not having let her sister in on her plan to escape. The strangest rumour pegged the woman as the author of the poet's lifework. The poet was the front, the chassis, while the mysterious woman was the true authorial engine.

During an interview for the *Globe and Mail*, the poet refused to confirm or deny any of the rumours, and she ended the interview when asked why she did not write more about what was obviously a very fertile and powerful personal past. A growing number of her readers, stimulated by the mystery, believed the poet already had. Though very few explicitly scoured her poems for evidence of the truth, most could not help hearing echoes of her past, sub-voices rising out of her work's sewers that murmured accounts of ancestral repressions, banished inheritances, personal curses. Didn't this meditation on the etymology of "alcohol" speak obliquely to the deeds of a domineering father? Didn't this lyric on the Virginia Tech shooting articulate guilt over abandoning her mother? Every poem was a portal, every image a clue. Responding to the story's surprising legs, an online indie rag announced their plans to dedicate an issue to the encounter between the poet and the mysterious woman. They put out a call for submissions seeking "poems, stories, videos, comics, polemics, flash games, prayers, oil landscapes, tattoos, spells, etc." inspired by the twenty-second clip and the four images of the poet huddling into herself on the floor at the foot of the stage.

* * *

No one turned to the Poem for evidence of the poet's past, and never again did the Poem come that close to being read in public. In fact, the time of the Poem's very minor presence in the world was growing short. At a Dadaist party held at the University of Calgary to raise funds for the English Student Association, a cut-up version of the Poem was mashed together with the Body section from Marvell's "A Dialogue between the Soul and the Body" and the chorus of a popular CeeLo track. The Poem also heavily influenced a piece in a self-published collection of *Star Wars*–themed poems, in the section professing to be Luke Skywalker's juvenilia, though Bob A. Fet, the author, did not admit this influence in his acknowledgements. One of the poet's more highly regarded colleagues at UNB was struck by the Poem's very corporal description of a minaret and he wondered, if the poet had a more global reputation, whether or not that description would warrant a fatwa. He began a story exploring this speculation but tossed it when the research led him elsewhere.

Most notably, the Poem inspired the managing editor at *The Varsity* to write a post on his blog titled "I Hate Poetry!" The post received over three thousand hits, a handful of Facebook thumbs-ups and a pair of retweets. The managing editor had been approached by a group of his fellow students who wanted to reboot the Poetry Corner in the arts section of the paper. To supplement their proposal, the students had submitted photocopies of old issues to provide a sense of their project's heritage. Reviewing the proposal, the managing editor's frustration had grown poem by poem until, five pieces in, he reached the Poem and had had his fill. What he hated about poetry, he shared on his blog, was how you had to read into it. He included a stanza from the Poem mid-rant to prove his point. It was a confusing passage about binoculars and birds he had found particularly disturbing. "I mean, I get it," he wrote, "at the basic level, but it's like the main point is to make you feel stupid." The stanza on the screen was stripped of its fellow stanzas and maker, its fellow poems and page, its name and what it named. Now, the managing editor concluded, was the age of "If you've got something to say, just say it!" Now, "[t]hings change so fast it's immoral to mix up the facts with metaphors and 'meanings' (and whatever the hell else these bastards are after)."

That was the Poem's last appearance. Unless you count the time the poet misremembered the Poem. She was on a day trip to a bird sanctuary organized by the Rec Tech at the senior's home she had lived at since turning eighty-three. The AI caregiver who guided the poet through the fluttering and chirping holograms asked if such vigorous life inspired her to write and the poet said yes. Once, she had even composed a poem about a man who watched birds from a rooftop, and his wife was there, too, and it was the poet herself who had given them the means to see those critters anew. Or maybe the Poem last appeared when the strain of payments and pain wiped out the clearing one of the Poem's descendants had opened inside a reader when, reading into the poem, the poem had read into her. Or maybe the Poem last appeared in the thick clouds of smoke that rose from the blaze that destroyed the last copy of the last book to hold the Poem. Or in the eyes that struggled from miles away to discern the origin of those flames. Or in a totally unconnected convergence of sense and distance, of gaps expanded and gaps smashed, as a different set of irises dilated to catch a different passing of a different form in flight.

YEAR ZERO

I WAS EXPECTING A DIFFERENT PACKAGE. ON SUNDAY, I had ordered an exceptionally rare Cambodian comic book, paying the online seller twenty-five bucks extra for next-day delivery. Still comic-less four days later, I went to bed certain I'd been scammed. So, this morning, when I woke to the sound of my landline ringing one last time as someone tried to buzz up, I threw on a housecoat and hurried to the lobby to catch the UPS delivery guy before he, and my Khmer Rouge–era comic, got away.

At ground level, no UPS employee peered through the frosted glass, no van darted into the slushy rush hour traffic on King Street West. A middle-aged woman, plump with layers, shivered in the late December cold, holding her white cane to her chest and clutching her hijab tight against the bursts of wind-powdered snow. Beside her, a cabbie rubbed his sweatered arms as he squinted at the condo's directory, trying to determine if he had punched the wrong code. The woman's last name was Ahmed.

I don't remember her first name. I met her once, at her daughter's funeral, but I recognized her as soon as I saw her face.

She had the same lips as Najwan, the bottom much plumper than the top, and, like Najwan, the corners of her mouth dropped so severely when she was distraught that it warped into the shape of a boomerang what was, when still, a very elegant mouth. Mrs. Ahmed had the same high cheekbones and narrow chin as her daughter, too, though these features had been rounded by years, swollen slightly, as though she were Najwan, post–bee sting.

The cabbie caught me watching from the foyer and gave a hopeful wave. I had to fight the urge to ride the elevator back up to the safety of my concrete burrow. Mrs. Ahmed lived north of where I taught, the University of Toronto Scarborough, so I knew her visit was urgent – the ride downtown having set her back at least a hundred bucks. The cabbie added a pleading smile to his desperate wave. The smile I tried to return died quickly. Any stab I took at faking faltered at the thought of the storms this woman could unleash. My intestines threatened to free-fall, to make themselves a fleshy rope, knotting further my already immobile feet. The cabbie alerted his fare to my presence.

"Professor Tysdal?" Najwan's mother ventured, her words muted by the glass.

"Yes," I said, hurrying to the door and pushing it open. "Mrs. Ahmed, how are you?"

"Freezing," she said, her words inflected with her accent's lilt, "but pleased you remember me."

"Of course, I remember you," I said. "I've been meaning to get in touch."

"Your time is valuable, Professor. I expect you had many big responsibilities."

"But I promised, at the funeral, to see if I could answer any questions you might have."

"Perhaps we could talk inside?"

"Yes, sorry. Please come in."

I tempered my invitation upstairs with a comment about the disorder of my loft. She graciously declined my offer, not wanting to waste, as she put it again, my valuable time. I was so on edge I wondered if she kept referring to my time as "valuable" because she knew I planned to waste the day binging *The Outer Limits*, *The Twilight Zone* knockoff I had picked up for myself on Blu-ray for Christmas. She asked the driver to wait, and then agreed, yes, it would be best for him to return to his cab and restart the meter. Business was always tight.

As the cabbie scampered back into the cold, Mrs. Ahmed confessed she was pressed for time herself. She had to hurry home to meet her sister and sister-in-law. They were helping her clean out Najwan's bedroom. Two years later, they had finally talked her into moving her daughter's things into storage, the compromise they had settled on when she refused to sell Najwan's possessions or throw them out.

"That is why I have come to visit you by surprise," she said, leaning her cane against her hip and reaching into her bag. "While we were cleaning, we found this."

She withdrew a sealed 10″ × 15″ catalogue envelope addressed to me. It was so stuffed Mrs. Ahmed needed both hands to hold it out for me to take.

"This is for you," she said, extending the envelope farther into the space between us.

"I'd better not," I said, "if Najwan had wanted me to have it she would have mailed it."

"Maybe she never had the chance."

"You and your family have the right to keep anything your daughter left behind."

"I insist."

"Really, I can't."

"Please!"

Her voice broke. She pushed the envelope so far forward she had to take a step to keep her balance, sending her cane to the floor with a crack. I knelt quickly and retrieved it. She took the cane from me. I caught the envelope as she let it drop into my hands.

The cramped printing was Najwan's. The letters of my name and of my home address were inked so closely together they looked like everlasting intimates, or inmates coerced to subsist in close quarters. I recognized her writing from the work she had submitted in my courses like "Creating Comics" and "Experimenting with Comics," and the yellow sticky notes she left on my office door – "I hope you're having a great day, sir," or "Dropped by to say hi, sir," crowded into word balloons emerging from the mouths of the amphibial, insect-like creatures she loved to invent.

"It was in with some things a friend of Najwan's returned after the funeral," she said, breaking me out of the envelope's hypnotizing gaze. "My brother's wife found it. Luckily, she asked me about it before tearing it open. My sister had to drive her home because she refused to stop whining, 'What's inside? What's inside?' That is why I regretfully had to disturb you so early. I wanted to give you the envelope before she brought my brother. He would have made me do it without your permission."

Hopeful, I took this as a cue. She really wanted to keep the contents of the envelope, but her honesty prevented it.

"You've done your duty," I said, "now let's have a look together."

"I don't want to know what is in there."

"I don't mind."

"I don't want to know."

Her hand reached out, the fingers of her winter-chilled gloves stilling my fingers against the envelope.

"We love our Najwan," she said, her eyes welling up, "you know this, Professor, and we always – always – tried to do what was best for her. She trusted you. I know this. And if she trusted you, I trust you."

She turned to leave, the hard end of her cane striking the tile, then the door, with a sharp click. I reached out to help her to the cab, but she brushed my hand aside.

"I promise to call if it's anything important," I said.

"Call me if it brings you peace, Professor. Only then. Peace is the one thing I need."

* * *

In the elevator, I hit P2 instead of going straight up to my place on the fifth floor, the envelope pinned between my torso and my arm like a stolen painting. It was the wrong painting, though. That was the thief I felt like. With no fence to free me from my illicit spoils, I had to make a decision. Destroy the thing? Break back into the gallery and return the work to its spot on the wall? Or hang it in my home, learn to appreciate the aesthetic and technical properties of what I understood as property to pinch?

The parking level storage room was a collection of interconnected, six-foot-high cages. Some were empty except for a few weeping cans of interior paints with names like Roman Ruins, Lemon Tart and Samba. Another cage contained nothing but a framed velvet canvas that tackily preserved the wide eyes, pointy breasts and almond skin of a local's take on a tourist's vision of a resort-pocked nation's "fairer sex." Another was packed with the ghosts of recreations past – golf clubs, tennis racquets, croquet mallets, snorkel gear – while another confined "the replaced" – the replaced microwave, the replaced mini-fridge, the replaced speakers and amp. This was the storage space as holding cell, the final stop before disposal.

The overhead fluorescent lights, for reasons that remain unclear to me, were also caged, further restraining their weak glow, and making it hard for me to distinguish the storage space key from the rest of my tiny keys: mail key, desk key, the key to a bike lock bolt-cuttered to bits by some crook three summers past. Amid all my junk is where I had buried it, the box of Najwan's things. The things I saved. I don't mean personal effects. I mean the items you would expect a professor to possess: my copies of her old assignments, the hard copies I made of our email correspondence and clippings of the articles written after her life was taken, some in languages other than English. The story of her death had gone global for a few days. Then it was done. "No legs," as they say. That's all.

I unlocked the cage, placed the envelope on top and set to work pulling out item after item: suitcases, a dolly with a wonky wheel, mismatched lamps, the full-body Predator costume I had blown a fortune on but never ended up wearing for Halloween because the helmet made me claustrophobic. Normally, I took comfort in the parking level's thick, sweet scent of old exhaust. It's the complexity of the odour that is so attractive, the way it signals travel and home, departure and return. Plus, I grew up on a farm, so I associate the smell of gas, tractor diesel and the lawn mower's mix of petrol and oil with nature, with the earth. It recalled the upside-down ocean of a blue sky cresting a field's green, then golden and then harvested growth. It reminded me of the light bursting in sharp beams through the holes in the barn's tin wall, undertaking in the dark the luminous archaeology that makes petrified claws and trilobites and spearheads of all the airborne dust. This morning, though, the stink of the parking garage inspired nausea. It worked in cahoots with Mrs. Ahmed's intrusion, the envelope and my empty stomach to leave me feeling seven-years-old-and-three-hours-on-the-merry-go-round ill. Oddly enough, this feeling gave me an idea for my superhero comic, *The Swipe*. These ideas still came to me intermittently, even though I had quit drawing *The Swipe* years ago. The Swipe is strapped into a madman's amusement park ride, a "beyond the pleasure principle" Gravitron. He is about to be spun into mush when he gets a whiff of it, this stink of the killing machine's fuel, the residue of what the terminal ride had burned to wipe out those it had wiped out before him.

I finally freed up the three by three stack of BCW comic boxes. They stretched to the back of the cage, protecting the comics I had devoured when I was a kid and the collections I had ordered online since but had not gotten around to reading. Three rows in, I reached the box marked "Naj." I lifted the lid enough to stuff the envelope inside. I shut the lid tight and reburied that box behind the comics, the costume, lamps, luggage and dolly, though I would have preferred to use fast-hardening molten steel to stop me from ever returning to dig back in.

* * *

Do you get rattled? I mean, when something shakes you, do you stay shaken? If you're like me, there is this sub-body within your body that vibrates intensely after you have been disturbed or threatened or exposed or outright attacked, buzzing like a pipe saw on its way through an endless inch of alloy steel and drowning out even the most well-composed orchestra of equanimity and reason. This body, a mishmash of sensation and fantasy and senti-ment and reality, invisible to everyone outside you, yearns to take the controls of your flesh-and-bone body, to become known. It wants to captain a week-long bender whose spoils are a mysterious softball-sized lump on the side of your face and the contraction of a venereal disease. Or it wants to shut your engines right down, impound you in bed and release you only for bathroom breaks and to hastily refuel on un-nuked microwave pizzas.

Returning from the storage room in the parking garage, I could feel this body birthing beneath my skin, maturing rapidly from the baby-sized ball of sickness in my gut to a full-fledged nervous system–distending force with a voice urging, "Get the envelope. Get the envelope." Admitting you have a problem, they say, is the first step to recovery. My problem with this adage has always been this: after I admit I have a problem, whether an addic-tion, a sickness or an obsession, I deal with it by bowing down to this problem's reign so I can come to know it fully in all its edicts, glories and whims.

A headache bloomed, one of those caffeine-withdrawal doozies that simulate an ice pick lobotomy. I made a quick cup of instant coffee to keep it in check. Fresh mug in hand, I took a seat on the toilet on the main floor, pants at my ankles even though I had no urge to go. It was a preventative gesture, like the wolf man who cuffs himself in a cage before every full moon. How much life-altering damage had been done by men seated on the can? I mean, historically speaking. I took a big swig of coffee, chewing the crystals the lukewarm water had not dissolved. I caught a glimpse of myself from the nose up in the bathroom mirror. Maintaining firm but cautious eye contact, I mentally broke the situation down for my reflection in the simplest terms possible.

After this semester, the twelve-week term set to begin in eleven days, I will have the summer to prepare and submit my promotion dossier. Forgetting the envelope equals committing to my present success equals a secure job at UTSC for the rest of my life. Obsessing over the envelope equals falling back into past bad habits equals, at the age of thirty-five, heading back to Starbucks or Chapters or Philthy McNasty's and fighting to publish indie comics, incapable of keeping a roof overhead or chewed up instant coffee in my belly.

My reflection in the mirror cut my anxiety-riddled counsel short.

"Sellout," it spit.

I flinched but did not turn away.

"Quitter," my reflection sneered, "you fake."

I stood up from the toilet to confront its abuse, its accusation, its mantra, "Sellout, quitter, fake. Sellout, quitter, fake." As I brought my face closer to the mirror, the intensity of my reflection's chanted charge increased until I was so intimate with its barely audible shriek the material reflected in the glass looked less like the features of a face and more like a heap of dough beaten by an invisible Mixmaster. An un-felicitous calculus obsessed my unconscious: if X does not open the envelope and let the envelope differentiate X into pieces, then Y will massacre the coordinates in which the envelope and X exist. I charged out of the bathroom and made another cup of coffee, this time waiting until the kettle squealed. I was that other werewolf, the one who controlled the lunar cycle and was this close to shouting to the full moon, "Rise!"

I decided to give the beast freedom in my office, the north-facing room on the second floor of my loft. With this mere sliver of control, the beast snickered with sick joy at the thought of tossing my computer through the window and filling my home with the blizzard that erased from view the roofs of townhouses, the roofs of old houses not yet levelled to make room for more townhouses and, beyond that, the denuded branches of the tallest trees in Trinity Bellwoods Park, which, if the beast could have seen them, would have manifested as the skeletons of mushroom clouds. My hope was to quell the urge for the envelope with some virtual marauding. The beast sent a noxious email to the seller in Vancouver who failed to deliver my Cambodian comic book, including with the invective multiple links to the definition of the phrase *next day delivery*. The beast took on the students who – in their timeless quest for an easy elective – had written me to request syllabi for the Winter term. Rather than admitting I had not started prepping, the beast composed epic syllabi characterized by ten-thousand-page reading lists, multilingual assignments and three-hour presentations performed in groups of fifty. The beast visited indie comic forums, and finding the rare thread discussing my work, attacked my attackers and gave my defenders hell.

The e-ssault was not enough. The manic urge to rip the envelope open remained, the urge to retrieve the envelope and let whatever it contained rip me open. Those emails were the equivalent of trying to quench a baby Gargantua's thirst for the milk of seventeen thousand, nine hundred and thirteen cows with a SlimFast 3-2-1 Plan Low Carb Diet Ready-to-Drink Shake. I paced my office, coughing so hard I nearly vomited. I paced more, expanding my route to include my bedroom, the stairwell and then the main floor, where I grabbed a carton of milk to subdue the burning acidity of the java. As my coughing worsened, transforming into a genuine dry heave, I worried I had eaten the envelope. Was my memory of caging the envelope a screen for what I had really done? What if I had, in fact, swallowed the envelope bite by bite to consume and dispose of it in one efficient act? The thought turned my stomach that final, fateful notch, and I darted back into the can and buried my barking head in the bowl. No shreds of paper floated in the milky ejected mess.

I turned to *The Outer Limits* for salvation. I sought liberation through numbness, freedom through immersion in cultural swill. The four episodes on the first disc couldn't save me. As they beamed on my screen, I sent apology emails to my students, admitting the baroque syllabi were a prank I played on industrious pupils. I heated up leftover pizza. I closed, opened and re-closed the curtains over the windows on the main and second floor, shutting out the blizzard, which had let up but still resembled the frozen locust plague sent by a miserable bunch of winter gods. I endured in my quest for sanctuary in *The Outer Limits*, though, and halfway through the second disc it worked. I was the drunk who wanted to forget the terrible mistakes of his parents, and to forget the terrible mistakes he had made trying to forget the terrible mistakes of his parents, by consuming drink after drink. I consumed episode after episode and I was soon soothed by the black-and-white images, the hacky storytelling, the rumbling cymbal of the theme song and the Control Voice in the voice-over warning at the start of each episode: they controlled this transmission, they controlled the sharpness of the image, they controlled the horizontal and the vertical of my television set. It was comforting, that feeling of nostalgia, of nostalgia for a very specific nostalgia that could never be mine. I felt like I had plopped down into one of the hammocks dads used to tie between trees in one-panel comics and family comedies. I was secure in this longing to feel lonesome for a time I was never, and could never be, an exile from.

By the fourth disc, I transcended that feeling – transcended feeling, really – achieving a tele-medial singularity, unmediated immersion, the viewing equivalent of the pugilist's punch-drunk, *dementia screenistica*. This was the true real, the real truth, the

pain and doom and fury of these aliens and outsiders and technologies and monsters: the scientist transformed into an alien
to unite world powers against a common enemy and end the
Cold War, the professor whose unconscious takes charge of his
mind-control implant and commits unspeakable acts, the time-
travelling mutant who returns to our era to stop the human-made
plague that deformed him, the Martians who visit Earth to study
humankind's peculiar penchant for murder. Reality was a ruse.
The twittering of tree-concealed sparrows, the kitchen thick with
the aroma of roasting garlic, the visible bursts of breath as one
friend stilled in the cold confides in her most vital companion,
the sublime gap that yawns between ascending airplanes hitting
their ceilings and sinking subs reaching the deepest depths of
the ocean floor, the hypnotic patterns of skin cells and arabesque
wallpaper, the mingling shadows of escalator-bound commuters
cast by the rising sun on the train station's far wall – all of these
details were designed, or devised, or evolved to conceal the total
reality of this very program. *Life* is the mere episode. *These episodes*
are Life. The one good act, the only good life, was to reproduce
these residents of the outer limits, to witness them, to let them
totally occupy your consciousness and take control, as the Control
Voice said, until you could sincerely hail each creature's demand
to "take me to your leader" with the reply, "I take you to yourself.
You are it."

* * *

I have written to you before, though you have not read what I
wrote for you. And you won't read it. That was the first thing
I did when I woke on my couch at 1:00 a.m. Friday morning, the
Blu-ray's home screen composed of a collage of black and white,
rubber horrors and looping the first twenty seconds of *The Outer
Limits*' theme song. I came up here to my office, sat down at my
computer and moved the folder titled "After Naj" to the Trash.
"You cannot undo this action," I was warned when I hit Empty. It

is permanent. This emptying. Emptying actions cannot be undone. I clicked OK, and deleted forever the draft outline for my book about Najwan.

I created a new folder and named it "After Envelope." I opened a blank document and I started to write to you. I wrote about Mrs. Ahmed's surprise visit. I wrote about storing Najwan's unsent envelope in the basement. I wrote about having a meltdown instead of opening the envelope. And now I write this, 2:43 a.m. Saturday morning, twenty-four hours after beginning. I write this sentence, telling you I have not retrieved the envelope from storage. I write this sentence to let you know I wrote and write all of this for you. Whoever you are, reader, consumer, witness, you have been with me since Najwan died. No. I lie. You were with me well before then, intensely, but after she died you changed. Or what I wanted to say to you changed. Or what I had to say to you. How I had to say it.

What's in the envelope? I hope it contains more of what I already saved, more of what I know, more of Najwan's comics, more of her essays, or something a tad more personal, like a journal, though I can't imagine her being any more open than she was in her assignments or in her posts on Facebook and Blogger and DeviantArt. I know from chatting with her she wrote more comics than I have read. She liked drawing these collections of disconnected four-panel strips depicting the spectrum of a personal relationship, with her parents, for example, or her siblings, her artistic heroes, her religion. There was a strip about her older sister who, grounded, rearranged the furniture to thwart their mom's mental map of their home. There was a strip about Najwan not really getting what it meant that her mom was blind until she witnessed the reaction of her kindergarten classmates. In the most powerful strip, she asks her mom if she regretted being blind. Her mom said, "No," she had a rich life and, she was certain, a good enough grasp of most sight-based elements, including faces, dimensions and colours, though she did confess she wished she knew what people meant when they talked about different "shades."

What do you think is in the envelope? Would you share? If I drew four blank panels on this page, would you draw what you thought? If you have a bunch of different theories, draw them all. Divide the panels into as many pieces as you've got ideas. Or if you're one for suspense, you could depict the moment I tear the envelope open, zooming in panel by panel, and ending so close in the last panel no one can discern what I withdraw. Or zoom out until, in the last panel, the viewer witnesses the world from an impossible point in the void, my window an unshaded dot lost in a galaxy of unshaded dots.

Or perhaps I'm asking the wrong thing. What *is* the envelope? That's the real question. What sort of story will unfold from the origin of its opening? What sort of hero will emerge? The envelope could be the alien child crash-landing on Earth after his parents rocketed him free from an exploding planet. The envelope could be the radioactive spider that bites an unsuspecting hand. The envelope could be the bat that bursts through the mansion window, inspiring the orphan to choose chiropteran features to form his new, crime-fighting identity.

I don't mean to delay or to be a tease. I really don't know what is in the envelope. And I don't want to know, not yet, anyway. Whatever she sent me will force me to confront my failures, my wrongs, even if the envelope contains blank pages, or the book I wrote and published in an alternate dimension Najwan miraculously visited and returned from. I will open the envelope in the morning, a time you can reach quickly by passing your eyes over the blank space that follows these words, but a moment I hope will be delayed for me by a night of time-transcending dreams, or a peaceful sleep, at least, free of nightmares like the one I had while napping this afternoon, the lone break I took from writing to you. A leech had attached itself to my chest, right above my heart. I could not tear it off with my hands or slice it off with a knife. I tried my lighter, in an attempt to heat the leech into letting go, but its skin caught fire, and my skin caught, too, and that slick green thing remained stuck to me as we both went up in flames.

* * *

The envelope contains two items: a notebook and a homemade card.

The notebook – a Mead Five Star three-subject wire-bound notebook, to be more specific – belonged to my UTSC colleague Dr. Thomas Buchanan Merrow, the man you know from the news as Najwan's attacker. The words *Mead* and *Five Star* are worn to a faint silver dust on the black plastic cover. Tom, a scholar of twentieth-century American literature from Montana, made his first entry in the notebook in the spring of 2009. The cardboard back of the notebook, half torn off the wire rings, is veined with lines where the cardboard cracked and folded. Tom traced these lines over in black ink, so they resemble rivulets of valuable minerals on a cave's stony terrain, or the flashing forks of a quiver of lightning bolts halted in their Zeus-thrown form. I have flipped through the notebook. A simple journal had been its initial purpose. However, as Tom's obsession with Najwan grew, the notebook also grew, becoming a storehouse for all things Najwan: a scrapbook for mementos, an archive for her marks and remarks, a testing ground for the book Tom had started to write about her, their relationship.

I have no idea how Najwan came into possession of Tom's notebook, but, as her card discloses, the notebook motivated her escape. The front of the card is wordless, decorated with one of Najwan's cryptids – a sickle-tailed one-eyed creature with the wings of a bat and a tiny, fanged mouth that, opened wide, is about one-tenth the size of the eye. Speed lines suggest the creature is about to fly off the edge of the card and escape into whatever awaits it in the world beyond the card's wing- and eye-decorated border. Inside the card, Najwan wrote about feeling a little scared by what happened with Tom, upset by his notebook, but, more than this, she felt liberated by the whole ordeal – inspired to venture out on her own, empowered to create the creative life she knew in her heart she needed to live. She already had a job at a comic shop lined up, thanks to my reference, and a place to stay with a former UTSC student who was doing grad studies out west. She concluded her message by entrusting me with Tom's notebook.

That was the word she used: *entrust*.

She wrote *trust*, too.

"I trust you to do with the notebook whatever you think is best, sir."

"I trust you," she wrote. Her mom's word, too: *trust*.

In classic Najwan fashion, she finished, "You will be rewarded with 72 black-eyed virgins in paradise (Jokes! ☺)." She signed the card, "Your grateful student always, Naj." The card is dated Wednesday, December 1, 2010. That was the day before the attack, four days before she died.

Her story needs to be told. I had always thought someone else would tell it. I was certain the facts of Najwan's death would spread to artists of every ilk – creative non-fiction activists, sober novelists, splatterers of house paints on massive canvases, Hollywood producers with major pull, cynical minimalist poets, guerrilla graffitists, post-country but pre-robotronic steel guitarists, YouTube curators, the composer of mainstream operatic opuses, and on and on and on. And these vast acres of creators would be unable to resist the seed of insight into total injustice Najwan's story spread, the seed of a feeling of hope spurred at the thought of the woman and the world that could have been. And these artists would nourish work that exposed the Dark Age we had been cast into when this bright star was snuffed out, art that stoked a palace coup of the Ruling Absolute (Love over Hate! Hope over Fear! Fellow Feeling over Solipsistic Greed!), voices that inspired an end to apathy and acquiescence, crying to us, "Welcome life! Encounter for the first time the fragile multiplicity of experience, and re-script in the code of your spirit the buggy conscience of our kind."

It was more than mourning. When she died, I swelled. I transformed, exploded into miles and miles of Stone Age terrain, miles of lower paleolithic expanses scorched in a time of blight, darkened in a time of an inviolably eclipsed sun. Yet, within this pre-ancient wasteland one hominid endured, stoking a fire at the mouth of a cave, bearing this flame into the wild on branches in his quest to find others who would also preserve and spread this warmth and illumination. And following Najwan's initial kindling in the rushed and artless doggerel of news agency hacks and Botoxed talking heads, I waited for her story to blaze. I assumed the stoking would start with requests for interviews from serious journalists, or from popular sensationalists and socially conscious academics. I was ready to help them revive the fading flames, to give them whatever material they needed to compose the initial, illuminating work, whether an overly sensational "true crime" exposé with a hokey, pun-packed title, for example, *A Veiled Truth*, or a more academic offering with a hokier long-winded subtitle, like *Thomas Buchanan Merrow, Honour Killed, and the Dark Side of the Western University.*

These journalists never came. No one did. The high point has remained the story published in the *Toronto Star* a week after Najwan died in hospital. A former UTSC student, interning with the *Star*, wrote the piece "How the Plan to Silence Najwan Ahmed Failed." Her connections to the school gave her insight into the mechanics of Tom's attempt to frame Najwan's family, but she did not capture any of the story's real significance. Only the photo of Najwan that accompanied the article caused a stir. The former student had snuck into Najwan's hospital room against the family's wishes to take the picture, and a public debate ensued about journalistic ethics. The student was attacked for callous exploitation. She was defended for upholding her right to preserve good old-fashioned facts.

This picture of Najwan had too many layers for people to really see it. The layers of the coma and life-sustaining machines concealed her vibrancy and silliness and sadness and cunning. The layers of blankets covered a body misshapen by Tom's blows. The layers of bandages wrapped around her head hid the face a jar of sulphuric acid had scorched, erased – one eye destroyed, nose and lips effaced of shape and sense and tone. Death was a layer, too. It hid forever the future in which Najwan's face healed into the smooth, featureless features of that appalling sorority of acid-attack victims, the future in which she stared into us with wide-eyed desperation, pleading, "Never again," from behind a visage that appeared mask-like, even though it was really the opposite of a mask, the universal root of every particular human face, the base face desired by and achieved through the basest hate.

Beyond the *Star* article, the web publication of Najwan's comics is the other initiative worth noting. I started a blog and posted scanned copies of her work, both the autobiographical stuff and her weirder, creature-filled comic strip fables. The strip titled *The Children*, from which the one-eyed cryptid on the card in the envelope originates, was the biggest success. The story begins in 1915 with the children from an unnamed village in an unnamed country being conscripted to participate in the Great War. The military promises the children will not see action. Instead, they will serve as scouts on the borders of friendly cities, keeping a lookout for saboteurs. A new threat soon overtakes the village's anxieties about the war when they come under attack by a sickle-tailed, one-eyed flying monster. The creature kills adult after adult, driving its hooked tail into the stomachs of its victims. With a hide impervious to bullet or blade, the thing seems unstoppable. The villagers grow thankful for the war. Against this monster, their children would not have stood a chance. Twenty villagers are brutally disembowelled before they manage to trap the creature in a barn and burn the barn to the ground. Soon after this victory, the war ends, and the villagers receive good news: their children will be returning home, with all of them having survived except for one who went AWOL. The next morning, the military train pulls into the station to the applause of the villagers. The applause quickly dies, though, as soldiers bearing cages, not the children, exit the train. The comic ends with the soldiers opening the cages and setting the children free. They emerge, one-eyed and sickle-tailed, wings flapping, permanently bound to the shape the war forced them to take to best perform their duty. Desperate for love, the children seek out their parents. They descend wildly for a loving, fatal embrace.

The Children was a minor internet hit. Several comics and pop culture blogs shared it, and I received a hundred-plus emails asking me to post the next chapter. There was no next chapter, but I attempted to oblige. Working in Najwan's style, I wrote a follow-up about the well-intentioned doctor who invented the horrific child-transforming procedure, but I possessed neither the courage to commit the deception of publishing my work in Najwan's name nor the permission to publish it under my own name. Soon, the reposts of Najwan's comics were limited exclusively to the memorial site, wemissyounaj.ca, created by Najwan's best friend. The comments on this site never ventured beyond superficial recollections like "OMG she was soooo talented." Out of frustration, I finally shut the comic blog down, though you can still find samples of Najwan's work on We Miss You Naj, which continues to act as a forum for her friends and former classmates to post poems of celebration and lament, MS Paint tributes, personal remembrances and favourite photos digitally appended with condolences ("May our memories be our comfort") or edited famous quotes ("When a great woman dies, for years the light she leaves behind her lies on the paths of men").

No one has told the story that needs to be told. All this time, I've lied to myself, swearing someone else could. The truth is, no one else can tell our tale because no one else knows the truth. What is missing from the story of Naj's loss, her family's suffering and Tom's crime, what remains untold, is the role I played in building our story's world. Our world. A story. How much of my help ensured events unfolded to tell the best story possible? Was I more wrong in assuming Naj needed saving or in caring too much about how her trials might be saved on the page? Is the first step to recovery admitting I have a confession? Is the first step to confessing asking: Am I really the reason she's gone?

Or is the first step forsaking the protection of questions? Simply stating it?

I'm the reason.

She's gone.

We were a world – Naj, Tom and I – and I am the one remaining inhabitant, the lone survivor, the last man, with nothing left to do but write, word for word, word by word, the origins of the world that was, which are the origins of our world's end. The envelope is less a miraculous sign and more a doom-laden reminder: that's all, I'm it. The one I was waiting for is me.

* * *

I was supposed to attend an AGO symposium today, *Inside the Outsider Artist*, and speak as part of a round table titled "Comic Books from the Margins." I had promised in the summer to give a talk on *Chhnam Saun*, or *Year Zero*, a comic composed during the Cambodian Genocide that documented the horrors of the Khmer Rouge's reign of terror. The comic was created by an anonymous collective of imprisoned artists who went by the name New People, a term the ruling regime used to distinguish professionals, academics and urbanites from the Old – rural, true, ideal – People. The Communist Party of Kampuchea's attitude to the New People is best summed up by the motto "To keep you is no benefit. To destroy you is no loss." *Year Zero* would have been banished to oblivion had it not ended up in the hands of a formerly CPK-sympathetic Western journalist who fled the country in 1976. The journalist had had the comic translated and distributed in an effort to shake the West out of its apathy toward the incomprehensible massacre. The original is preserved at a former high school–turned–death camp–turned–museum in Phnom Penh, and both the 1977 translation and 1989 reprint are valued by serious collectors and thus rare. This past summer, all three of my attempts to purchase *Year Zero* turned out to be dead ends, and before I had a chance to investigate further the Fall semester consumed me. I had forgotten about my AGO talk until a week ago, when a promotional e-vite, complete with a poster with my name on it, reminded me of my promise and my search for *Year Zero* began anew.

Before receiving the envelope, I had intended to attend the symposium. In place of the presentation on *Year Zero*, I was going to give my usual talk on my own work, *The Swipe*, which adopted an intentionally "outsider" or *art brut* style. *The Swipe* was a parody of the teenager-turned–reluctant superhero genre. My unassuming teen journalist, Sterling Stoops, was transformed into The Swipe after sneaking past a police barricade to shoot exclusive footage of his university's telecommunications research facility consumed by flames. As Stoops made his way to a rooftop across the street, the fire grew in ferocity, and right as he captured footage of a blazing satellite dish, the facility exploded. Though the explosion evaporated Stoops's body, his consciousness was melded with his camcorder. The Stoops-Camcorder hybrid possessed the power to steal, or "swipe," the form and function of any living entity or inanimate object. The catch: this "swipe" could only take place when an external user pointed the camcorder at said subject and clicked Record. Composed entirely of "swipes," the comic mirrored its hero. I copied (and modified, of course, for the sake of continuity and copyright) characters, panels and full-page layouts from great strips and comics, often mashing up eras and heroes, Winsor McCay with Jack Kirby, Astro Boy with Archie Andrews, to illustrate The Swipe's epic quest to find a permanent human form while thwarting the evil machinations of his growing rogues' gallery: Mr. Original, Mage Marginal and Supraman.

Instead of attending the AGO symposium and giving a talk on my old work, though, I committed to telling Naj's story. I retrieved her box from storage, rearranged my office and started filing the materials from Tom's notebook. Skipping from task to task, penning to-do list after to-do list, I was a flock of sparrows alighting on the pavement, hopping their hollow-boned selves from morsel to morsel, pecking at crumbs, coins, cigarette butts, the dried poo of other fowl, their multiple hungers combining to form a single feasting being. Immersed in this important work, I did not feel a speck of guilt over not calling the symposium's organizer at the AGO to say I was bailing, though I did finally turn my cellphone off, the intervals between its rings diminishing as my three o'clock talk neared. I tacked up Najwan's card on the bulletin board to the right of my desk. I half-emptied and quarter-arranged the materials from the BCW comic box. I sat down to write this to you.

As I conclude these initial remarks and prepare to tell Najwan's story, to offer my confession, I realize it was deceptive of me to note the card in the envelope was written the day before Najwan was murdered. My statement implied she knew exactly what was coming. It implied she was helpless and passive, writing to me as though I were her only hope. She did, of course, know things had gone sideways with Tom, that was why she planned to leave the city, but she wrote the card and asked me to deal with Tom's notebook because she was cutting ties with the selves everyone else expected her to be, me included. She was escaping to create the self she wanted to become. She believed she was in the clear. She did not know Tom was coming. She did not know how he knew how to find her.

While I was writing to you, *Year Zero* arrived. My landline rang, I buzzed the UPS guy up and he delivered thirty-one photocopies of the Cambodian comic. It turns out an error in the credit card info I entered the first time around had stopped the initial order from going through. The seller in Vancouver had sent the thirty-one copies in response to my second order. Apparently, in between my toxic email's threats and insults, I had sarcastically remarked that his top-notch business must require high-volume orders, so I demanded a copy for every day of the coming month. The seller had obliged. He included an invoice to show I had been charged for each copy, and a note asking, "How's this for next fucking day?" The parcel had taken two days. That did not diminish his overall point.

Though I am finally committed to telling you Najwan's story, I will have to take a break tonight to read *Year Zero* (though *read*, I realize, is not the right word). I could hardly resist paging through it when I first opened the parcel. I just skimmed it again. It's all here in pencil, preserved first-hand. The forced exodus. The forced labour. The force-less teachers and monks and civil servants and literates and artists and merchants and families forced into the fields, force-fed mottos – "The sick are victims of their own imagination," "Better to kill an innocent than spare an enemy by mistake." Water, fire, tool – the base elements of civil life and biological order are turned against life and order, in the name of life and order. Stories are forced, forcefully transcribed, then the confessions are signed at gunpoint and then the gun is fired. It's all here, though sometimes sketched so quickly the panels and pain are seamed in senseless abstraction.

I am sickened to think I'd so carelessly offered to illuminate what should steer us straight into pitch-black. Any talk I might have given would have paled before what I'm looking at, the way hearing the word *moon* pales before witnessing the moon fall from the sky and crush you where you sleep. This is the kind of work (wail?) that gets you thinking about the miracle of its creation (not the right phrase) and you feel (wrong verb, I know) like you're having your lungs pulled out through your esophagus. It's the kind of thing you read (wrong) and wonder (wrong) how you will ever (wrong) at yourself in the (wrong) again.

WAVE FORM

This is a waveform.

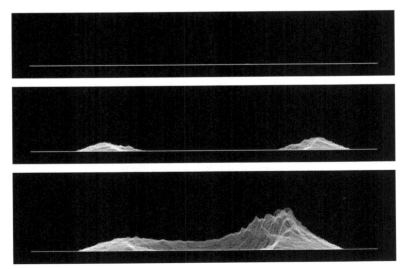

This is a waveform of a video-editing tutorial about waveforms.

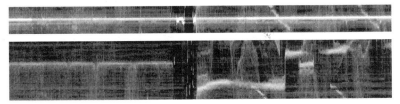

The instructor shows us how this type of waveform measures

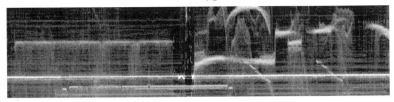

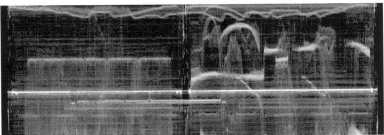

the luma of a moving image, what some might call its brightness or luminescence.

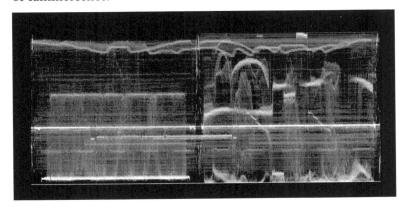

These are different waveforms of the footage I filmed of my friend, barely visible beneath the waving trees of the park.

This is a waveform of him telling me how, when his luminescence vanishes, he paces aching through this park, the waves of depression dragging him under.

These are different waveforms of the footage I shot from a subway platform, my friend waving to me as his train pulls in.

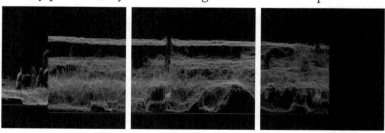

He admits that, when his brightness dwindles, he can't look down at the tracks without this sickness in him sneering, "Do it. Jump. Die." He can't stop his mind from welcoming inside all the ways he could end his life.

This is a waveform of the end of a movie that saved his life. It's Fellini's *La Dolce Vita*. The girl waves across a chasm to the failed hero, her message made indecipherable by the ocean's crashing surf.

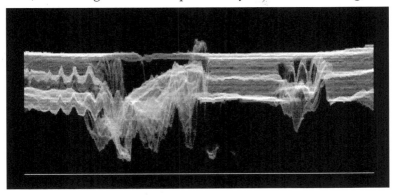

These are the waveforms of other cinematic waves that have helped my friend survive from boyhood to today.

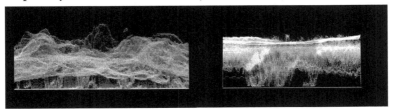

The waves of burly Hawkmen saving the day in *Flash Gordon*, and the tides of waste salvaged in Varda's *The Gleaners and I*.

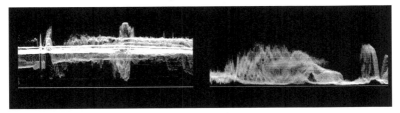

The gentle wake that trails the fin in *Jaws*, and the joyous surge of a teacher's embrace as Lale goes free in Ergüven's *Mustang*.

Here is the whirlpooling process and audience in *Man with a Movie Camera*.

The wave-shaped chalk that marks the murderer in *M*.

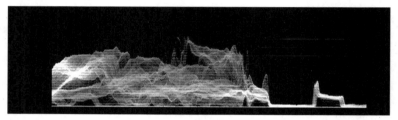

The surfacing of inner selves through angels in *Wings of Desire*.

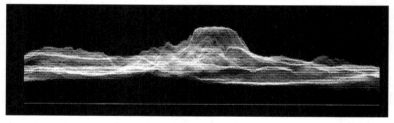

And the swimming lesson in *Moonlight*, offered in the middle of the world.

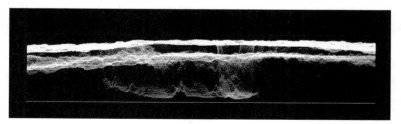

It's curative, the way these filmic waves accumulate: waves of

images and emotions, of insights and symbols. They lift us from our

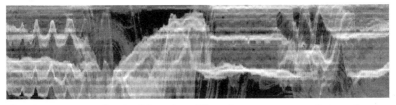

depths into sun-frothed heights. They ferry us to sustaining shores.

My friend seeks recommendations from companions who share this love of film, riding the waves that buoy them.

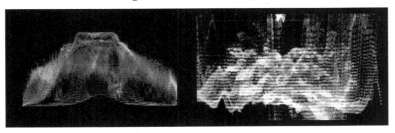

From Paola comes the wind-waved grass in Tarkovsky's *The Mirror*, which foreshadows fire.

From Noor: the waves of authenticity, illumination, resistance and play in Kiarostami's *Close-Up*.

From Nehal: the devastating waves in *The Perfect Storm* with their body-shocking sublimity and groundbreaking effects.

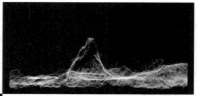

And from Oubah: the rippling waves of *mise en abyme*, pictures within the picture – Rose sketched in *Titanic*, or *Blow-Up*'s corpse photographed by chance.

I ask the love of my life to name an indelible wave, and she shares the disturbing awe spurred by *Apocalypse Now*'s "smell of napalm," by men like that untouchable lieutenant who can surf a war unscathed.

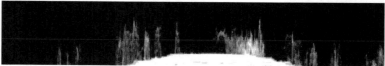

And my oldest friend? She offers Black vanguard cinema, which is wavy in the hip hop–culture sense of the word: creating your own path, being original, riding your own wave.

They envelop us as we watch, the waves of cinema's different times and lands and lives, the surges of imagination and the impossible.

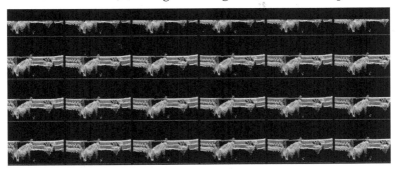

Movies march us through the murk, rally with the rich plenitude

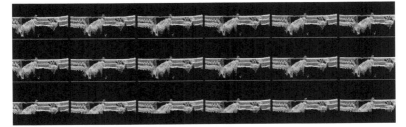

of the world: all the eras, regions and peoples quickened by these

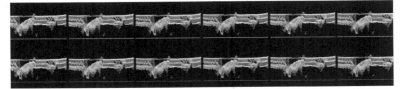

different eras, regions and peoples – multiplying meaning, expanding time.

My friend and I wish we knew which cinematic waves save you so we could include them here, too.

Do you long for Dorothy's ruby slippers beckoning home?

Or the walled-up waves of the parted Red Sea?

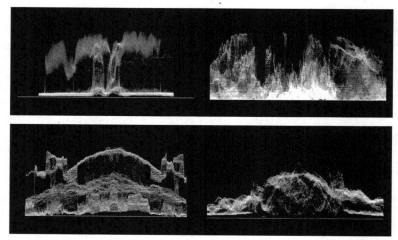

Or the shining crimson blood that deluges the hotel lobby?

Maybe the fluttering of Scottie's hair as he vertigos in the spiral of time.

Maybe the lips that wave goodbye with one final, inscrutable word:

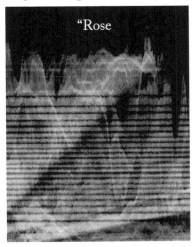

"Rose

bud."

Here, for some of you, is the dress undulating in *L'Atalante*'s magical underwater dance, and here, for others, is the billowing surge of zombie cars in *The Fate of the Furious*.

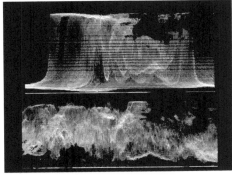

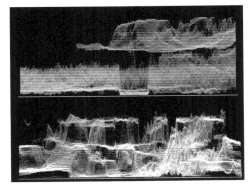

Here, for you, is the wave of Death's robe with his seaside arrival in *The Seventh Seal*, while here, for you, is the wave of Death's robe as he loses a game of Twister in *Bill & Ted's Bogus Journey*.

The waves of cinema's many transformations – the changing characters and twisting plots, the developing styles and the medium's

flux – spread like a spell of extreme weather, enclosing my friend in the climate of these preserving metamorphoses. This isn't an

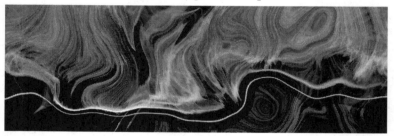

escape from the world. Movies are an immersion in the world: a downpour of fantastic truths and real fantasies we would

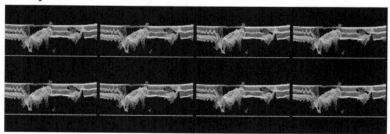

otherwise never be replenished by. A plunge into the vivified

longings and lives that flood the screen.

The wave of the movie you're reading right now, it saves my friend,

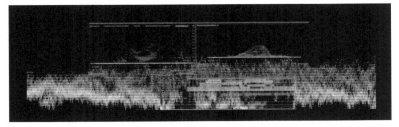

too. Here it is – a waveform of waveforms – playing again from

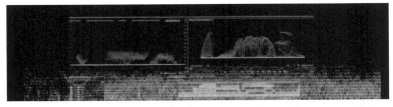

the start. This act of waving back to movies by making a movie is

a guiding wind. It bends my friend into focus, gives him direction

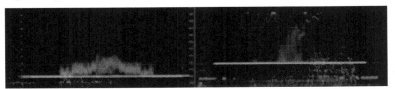

with history and art. These sustaining gusts never diminish, even

though what he makes is a pebble rippling waves in an alleyway
puddle, a puddle tossed into an ocean-rocking squall.

This is a waveform of my friend in close-up, working on this film.

Making this film is his way of waving to you, of waiting for you to wave back.

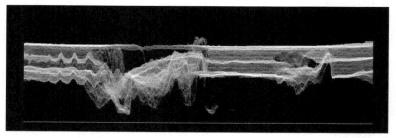

This is a waveform of him saying it's okay if you don't wave back, or never even see this to know he's waiting.

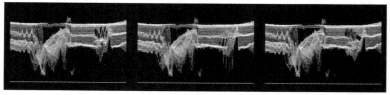

This wave is a measure of his luminescence, a brightening of his glow. Making it for you crests him above the urge to end all the

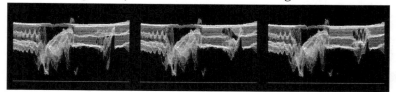

waves that remain in him to rise.

This is a waveform of my friend waving to you through the downpour.

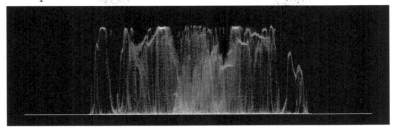

Waiting for you in the tumult.

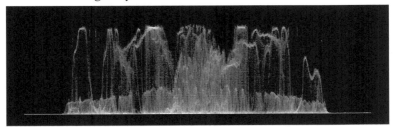

Holding the shape of a shore,

keeping the boat steady,

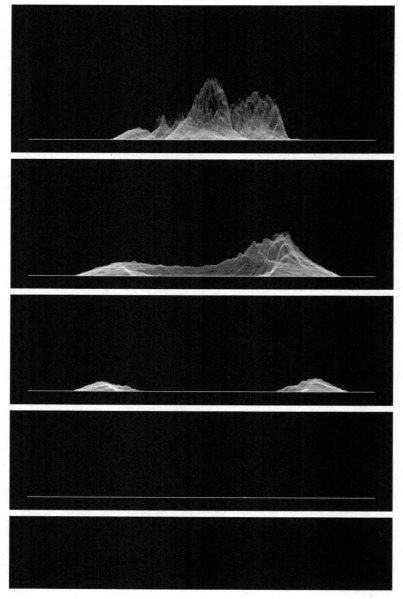

until we survive.

DOOM SCROLLS

And as imagination bodies forth
The forms of things well-known, the poet's pen
Turns them to shadows, and makes of names
And local habitation an airy nothing.
— Melancholy Jaques
Macbeth, 5.5.25–28

THEY ARE ALL ANONYMOUS.
The man who is about to jump.
The lens that will catch his fall.
The life this image ruins.
The hands whose clicks and taps will spur this ruin's spread.
The budding star who takes control of the subway train.
Her first solo drive.
Five years ago, after receiving her BFA in Theatre Studies and
a Class of 2006 Dean's Merit Award, she never would have guessed

she'd be dressing up in a transit uniform, or operating under a badge number, instead of preparing to play Celie Johnson in a musical revival of *The Color Purple*, or a female incarnation of "the Moor" in a gender-inverted adaptation of *Othello*, or, when she really caught her break, the irreverent lead in a sitcom that rewrites the formula and spurs spinoff after copy after homage after nudge-nudge-wink-wink reference in feature-length animated films pitched at parents and kids. She is meant to grace the ads on the sides of buses announcing the next prime-time hit, not operate the vehicles that spread the good word stop by stop by stop. She eases the train up to the subway platform for the first time, undershoots it by four feet. No one she can see through her window notices.

When her father called to tell her she had gotten the job, he had acted like she had won a lifetime achievement award at the Oscars. Speaking from thirty-plus years of public transit experience, he had promised she was about to embark on a well-paying and rewarding journey. Maybe thirty-plus years down the road she will say the same thing to her own failed child, but it will not be *her* making this promise. It will be the woman who remains after this job rewrites her dreams and revises her desires, producing the ultimate nightmare role, the equivalent of a stand-in for an extra in a straight-to-DVD low-budget thriller. An hour into this first solo shift, she can already feel herself being erased. The seat wears her. The accelerator grips her hand. The dead man's pedal coffins her shoe. The train is a costume commuters pull around themselves, and she is an invisible stitch, a piece the machine needs to gain speed but no more noticeable than the chime-sounding electronics or electricity-directing circuits. The bells pulse. The doors close. The train wills her to ease it out of the station.

The train surfaces, clattering out of the tunnel into the spring night. Metal fencing hems the tracks in. The backs of high-rises and then the valley's trees hem in the fence. Five times a day during her in-class training, and twice as many times during her in-vehicle training, she was told cellphone use is strictly prohibited while operating the train. This repeated warning is not enough. A knowledge and a faith circulates through her, a physiological consciousness of her destiny. She is meant to carry people, this she doesn't doubt, but the true vehicle is her talent as a performer, the real destinations are mind-expanding intellectual depths, sublime emotional heights and the simple, satisfying sense of being wholly entertained. There are three stops before the train hurls her back underground. Even though she knows it will end in a screaming match, she phones her mom to plead her case.

Her mom is also at work – her curt tone as much of a giveaway as the background clatter and shouts of the hotel kitchen. The curtains open on the argument the two of them have had again and again since the budding star was a little girl. It's her most regular gig, the most honest and gruelling. Her mom will ask her, again, what makes her think she is so special, and she will explain, again, this has nothing to do with being special. This has everything to do with being called, being called to perform. Imagine hearing your name chorused every second of every day and never being able to answer, "Yes?"

Her mom asks, on cue, "What makes you think you're so special?"

As the next station nears, their repeated scene repeats.

She does not notice her fellow anon, the man who is about to jump to the tracks. He clings in the dark to the side of the bridge, watching the train, at that distance quaint as a toy, pull to a stop in the station down the line. He has no ID. He didn't leave a note. It took industrial-grade metal cutters to clip through the fence erected to save the bridge from its nickname, "Loner's Leap," which it owes to the pain-erasing summoning of its forty-foot fall. He'd had to work quickly and discreetly, hoping the dark of the spring night and the speed of the vehicles would hide his intentions from the traffic passing on the bridge. He had let the first train to glide beneath him pass. It would have been too early. He checks his watch. The next one is it.

Back in the autumn, anonymity had not been a goal when he decided to end his life. He just hadn't wanted to do it alone. He visited a suicide discussion forum, hoping to find a like-minded companion with whom he could die. He stumbled upon a discussion thread titled "Don't you want your death to have meaning?" He joined the conversation. Later, he received a private message from the thread's creator, asking if he'd like to join The Nameless.

He didn't buy it, what the financial broker who founded The Nameless was selling. The broker had these highfalutin ways of putting it. Their deaths would have meaning through their total lack of meaning. How else to reach people a decade after 9/11? If you want your suicide to make a difference, then anonymity is necessary. If The Nameless all took their lives at the same time, in an attention-grabbing fashion, and did so without signalling a name or cause or motivation or belief, then their deaths could signal every name and cause and motivation and belief. The duties inspired by their raw "No" – by the purity of their resistance – would arise from the eye of the beholder.

"We will be saviours," the broker repeated, as did other members in moments of exhilaration, or sensing the doubt of the man who is about to jump to the tracks. "We will shock each individual who sees us into seeing things must change."

What had kept the man committed to The Nameless was the bond he shared with the group's first member, a former junior hockey star whose parents had kicked him out of the house and whose teammates had ridiculed him into quitting the sport he loved when they found out he was gay. The man and the former junior hockey star hit it off right away online, chatting virtually for hours about NHL minutiae, possible afterlives, the significance of their approaching sacrifice. The kid saw their deaths as, like, little suns to build new worlds around. The man had been inspired by the kid's description a thousand times more than any of the broker's abstract ramblings about anonymity and salvation. He would hint at his apprehension about the broker, but the former junior hockey star never once bit. Instead, he spoke of the broker with total admiration.

"I was nineteen, hooked on painkillers and this close to living on the street when we met," the former junior hockey star once typed.

"Now, for the first time in my life, I feel at peace, and I'm working with a wicked group of guys who are going to change the world."

The train finally pulls out of the station and accelerates in his direction, and the man who is about to jump to the tracks thinks of the former junior hockey star, thinks how thankful he is for the last few weeks when The Nameless moved into a house together. He bends deeply at the knees, flexes his arms. He tries to get a sense of the push he'll need to fall and hit the tracks. The broker bought the house partly to facilitate the final stages of planning – scouting potential locations together, providing support in sticking to the rigorous cleansing regime, determining how best to do it without harming bystanders – and partly to leave another empty sign in the form of the house vacated of everything but the basics, no letters or possessions or clues.

Thinking of the former junior hockey star, the man who is about to jump to the tracks feels it again, high above the earth in the cool night air, the train appearing less toylike as it nears. It's the feeling he felt when he first met the kid in person, reached out to shake his hand only to have the grinning man-child yank him into his broad chest for a mighty hug. His friendly affection for his online intimate had grown into fatherly love during their virtual chats, and meeting in person this feeling was confirmed and amplified, and, he knew, reciprocated. When they did chores together, conversed for hours or scouted locations, he understood this was the son he should have had, and he was the father by whom the kid should have been raised. No matter what, he would have done right by him. He would have loved him, no matter what.

The train nears, jangling like a spur. He can make out the form of the driver and he wonders if the driver sees him. Or is he merely a shape to that shape, an empty garbage bag the wind has tangled in the high fence? He wonders who at the hopping commercial district's intersection has spotted the former junior hockey star. Did a retired colonel recognize the bulge beneath the kid's jacket as an explosive? Did the colonel reach out to stop him before the boy ascended the billboard and blew himself up? Who at the mall,

the science centre, the war monument, the house of God is inno-
cently watching one of The Nameless right now, right before they
do it, with bomb or blade or gun or leap into empty air? Is a police
officer at the baseball stadium eyeing the broker in the front row?
Or had a catcher diving for a foul ball crashed into him, setting
off his bomb too soon and killing innocent fans? That was the
darkest day with the kid. A few of them drove out to the woods
to test the explosives, to make sure the detonation wouldn't be too
big. He heard the blast, but he couldn't watch. He stared at the kid
who should have been his son, the one he loved, unable to fathom
this bright light being snuffed out in such a senseless, brutal way.
This is what he sees as he lets go of the bridge, his eyes closed: that
lovely, loving face.

The sixteen-year-old girl who runs the website on which the
photo of the fallen man's mangled body will appear is anonymous
in the way centuries-old authors are anonymous – the poet who
penned, "The outlanders pursue him as if he were game," or the
first monk to ask, "Who is it who drags your corpse around?" Her
anonymous creation is the website I-Chat, short for ignatius-
chatter.com. The website is an imitation of her all-time favourite
imageboard, 4chan. She has been around computers since she was
a little girl and I-Chat, though her umpteenth website, is her most
ambitious undertaking: an attempt to replicate on a local scale
4chan's global revolution.

When the site was completed last year, she sent anonymous
emails from her I-Chat account to an assortment of influential students at Ignatius High, inviting them to join. As word of the site
spread, more of her classmates requested passwords by sending their
student numbers to an email address provided on the home page.
Once signed on, her classmates could post in the various forums:
/h/ for homework, /a/ for athletics, /p/ for parties, /r/ for rumours.
A half-dozen volunteer mods began working under her for the sole
reward of a few scraps of her power. Over the last few months, she
has been accepting requests from students from schools all over the
north end. The whole city, she is certain, will be next.

She doesn't think of I-Chat as the voice she was missing at school. It's more a net to catch the voices of her classmates, the whistle and the rink with which to direct their play. She decides which threads make the main page, which threads are deleted, which IP addresses receive the ban-hammer for crossing which line. The site became so popular so quickly that even the teachers who blocked it from school computers and promised it would be shut down soon knew to call it I-Chat. The obsession continues to spread through the genuine glee of the infected initiates. It is an easy sell. If you want to know who is scrapping after school, you check I. Hear a rumour about your boyfriend? Confirm it on I. You want to force the creep in Woods Class, the front-row know-it-all in English, your best-best friend 4eva!! to transfer schools? Post what you caught them doing on I. Everyone is watching and waiting to act on what they witness.

It is all anonymous. That is what sets it apart from the other social-networking groups, email accounts and web forums her classmates community through. None of them know who created the site. None of them know who posts which text and which image. There are no avatars or nicknames. No accounts to personalize with "My Favourite ____" lists, or a digital doll to dress in purchasable digital wear. There are no barriers or distinctions: no classrooms or class, no gender or creed, no race or reputation. Anonymous reveals Amber S. is sucking more than one dick. Anonymous updates: the party in the valley is moving to the lake. Anonymous posts pics of Miss Hay's panty line from French class. Anonymous is -_- and >:-) and :-O. Anonymous demands, "Tits or GTFO!"

When the image of the man mangled on the tracks first appears on I-Chat, accompanied by the words "YOU WILL NOT BELIEVE WHAT I FUCKING SAW TONIGHT," the sixteen-year-old girl does not witness its arrival. She is on her way downstairs to attend an inter–high school superhero-themed costume party organized by Ignatius's video game club. Sexy Pirate is usually her go-to costume, because it is always such a hit, but she is sick of having to reveal to the kids from other schools the secret to her authentic-looking wooden leg. Her "secret" is the truth: a boating accident when she was three. The blade of the motor shredded her leg into pieces and what didn't sink to the weedy bottom of the man-made lake held an unrepairable shape. Tonight, she goes with Sexy Superwoman: a cape and miniskirt she made from red duct tape, her prosthetic leg decorated with paint and tinfoil to simulate an attack by Brainiac and a blue bustier complete with her take on the Superman logo stitched to the front, the traditional *S* replaced by the wheelchair-riding universal symbol of access.

"Shameful," her mom gasps, instantly.

"You're shameful for calling me shameful," she counters. "You're supposed to raise children, not constantly judge them."

"If only I were so powerful," her mom snaps. "You head right back upstairs and change, missy, or you are not leaving this house."

Her mom's strike spreads an electric shiver along the sixteen-year-old girl's spine and arms, from her shoulders to the hands she clenches to shake it away, a rage-rich burn tightening in her heart and stomach as though the two rulers of her insides are doing battle or trying to fuse into a new, unsustainable organ. The sensation of hate flourishes with such intensity, as sensations always do in her – sensations of pleasure, of pain, of hope, of failure – that she will not be surprised if it turns her skin and bone and musculature translucent, disbanding all that is not a nerve, until the sensation holds its form naked in the air, taking the shape of timbers leaned together at the top, penning in the early embers of the wildest fire.

"Fuck you," she screams, and repeats it, like a chant, "fuck you, fuck you, fuck you."

She keeps the mantra going as she ascends the stairs, stumbles into her bedroom and slams the door, clamping the two locks tight.

She gathers herself on the floor. Her panting becomes deep breaths, and as she moves to her computer she catches a glimpse of herself in the mirror. Her red tape skirt conceals the border of plastic and skin where the mock-attacked prosthesis joins the curve of her upper thigh. What her mom sees, she guesses, is a well-armed and fanatical sentinel who holds her real daughter captive. Even when they're getting along, her mom assesses, judges, critiques and scolds. "Constructive coaching" is her mom's phrase for it, speaking as though she were attempting to sneak a message past a severe warden to the prisoner closeted in the cell of a vault far, far, far underfoot. The sixteen-year-old girl sometimes believes she is an inmate: to her mom, to her disability. She feels like her leg hasn't been lost but pushed into her squat stature, and the extra girth with which it fills her stomach, breasts, cheeks and thighs is a fettering cage, thwarting her every effort to reach out, calling off the search party tasked with locating any gesture from the real world that might possibly reach out for her. It's why she built the site: to reach and to be reached.

Her mom knocks on her bedroom door with a peace offering.

"You can wear my bumblebee costume if you'd like."

"I'm not going out."

After a long silence, her mom asks, exasperated, "What are you trying to prove?"

"Everything, Mom, every fucking thing."

"What the hell is going on? Are you some kind of goth? Are you an emo?"

"No, Mom. I'm something you'll never be."

"What's that?"

"Loved."

The sixteen-year-old girl is loved. She does not have to respond to her mom's demand that she open this door right now. She has another home, another family, one that frees her to ignore her mom's pounding, her muttering departure down the hall. The girl settles into the chair in front of her computer. She logs onto I-Chat. She goes straight to /f/ for feels.

"I'm so fucking sad, I-Chat," she posts anonymously, "cheer me up."

Anonymous replies, "I'm so sorry," "Sending you positive vibes," "What's up?" Anonymous posts images of cats and kittens, a "bawww" comic to show solidarity, a rainbow-backed marijuana plant with the offer to meet up for a j and a meme that always makes her lol: an image of Patrick Stewart with the quote "Use the force, Harry" attributed to Gandalf. Anonymous keeps coming through, until it doesn't. An image of a decapitated head appears. It's the work of a troll, or, as one Anon puts it, "Obvious troll is obvious." The troll, or another troll, posts an image of a decomposing obese woman, trying to inspire shock or rage or sadness, any manner of reaction. A troll posts an image of a pile of meat, no, a body mangled on train tracks, the rear of a subway car visible in the background.

As with her site's animus, 4chan, the most controversial forum is /b/, random. /b/ is where anything goes. It is dedicated to strangeness, absurdity, porn, hate and, hardest for her to handle, gore: the Chinese criminal de-limbed a century ago flanked by the mob that got him, a mound of Holocaust victims, the bloated corpse of an OD'd comedian, a pair of self-terminated high school shooters and the androgynous body mangled on the tracks.

This is a new one. The two transit deaths previously posted on I-Chat take the form of surveillance footage shot overseas by ceiling-mounted cameras: an old woman in China hurries onto the tracks as though late for an appointment with an impatient ancestor, and an Indian man emerges from beneath the platform and rolls in front the oncoming train, starfishing on the rails before the unbreakable surf of steel takes him away. The preservation of the latest victim is different. Instead of footage, there are stills, taken up close, after the collision. The person who shot these was standing on the tracks. A few of the sincere anonymous I-Chatterers reply, "How awful," "Keep the gore in /b/!" and "So tragic ☹ RIP." These sparks of disgust and pain are fed further by the trolls, who proceed to dump more gore and more versions of these cellphone images with words they've Photoshopped atop: "Why your train was late," "Delicious steak!" and "Could I get a transfer?"

For the sixteen-year-old girl these word-brutalized images are like a ghoulish Spider-Man web-slinging through the peaks of the skyscrapers of her memories, touching this one and this one and this one, their existential or structural or spiritual fellow-travellers:

her memory of other www-framed and frozen bursts of gore, her memory of the Elm Street movie where Freddy fed the girl her own intestines, the tire-crushed head of a squirrel, the menstrual clumps her mom had forgotten to flush years and years ago, her memory of the plasticity of clouds, of porridge, traffic-sailed snow, the comic strip one I-Chatterer had posted in /a/, art, about a seventeenth-century Jesuit who fed the bodies of murdered Haudenosaunee to the Haudenosaunee he converted, making, as the priest cried out in the final frame, "the living holy with the body of a holy dead." It had been called *The Host* or *The Bred*. She can't remember, but she is sure the images of the person mangled on the tracks could pose for a panel.

She hits F5 to refresh the screen, and the newly accumulated responses from the I-Chatterers load in a flash. The trolls have added more gore. Normally, she loves her trolls, and is one of their leading members on other sites, but as I-Chat's webmaster she has other responsibilities, order to uphold, and the transgression cannot stand, especially not with the night she's had. She deletes the thread. It is the game of God and mouse she and the trolls play. They always lose and learn. She keeps them contained to /b/. The ones who post shocking content where it does not belong – an image of a porn star with a ten-inch cock getting rimmed, or the gif of Al Qaeda Super Mario bringing down the Twin Towers – soon learn who rules the rules. A twenty-four-hour ban does the trick.

What the sixteen-year-old girl doesn't know, as she deletes the thread, is the hardcore troll is watching over her. She does not know that, for the hardcore troll, the hubris she displays in this deletion is the last straw. He will now delete her.

The hardcore troll's pursuit of the sixteen-year-old girl commenced a week ago. The sixteen-year-old girl had visited the /b/ forum on 4chan and posted a rallying cry, "/b/tards unite!" In her post, she disclosed her principal at Ignatius High had threatened to cancel the spring formal if I-Chat, her own 4chan-inspired site, did not cease operations. She demanded /b/ defend her work by hacking her principal's email account and sending bestiality porn to everyone on his contact list. Once this had been accomplished, she would post instructions regarding the next phase. /b/ had replied, collectively, in the negative, though this *no* had taken many different forms:

"/b/ is not your personal army."

"I'LL FUCK YOUR SPRING FORMAL IN THE ASS AT FULL FORCE."

"Tits or GTFO."

As the *no* had grown in duration and ferocity, the sixteen-year-old girl had lashed out, accusing those /b/tards of being fakes, phoneys, cowards, fuckers of mothers, shiteaters.

"One day, I'm going to make you regret this, /b/," she had written. "You have failed your future queen!"

Raging at this nobody's inflated sense of self-importance, the hardcore troll had rallied a group of similarly raging trolls. He had coordinated the prelude to their attack, delegating duties: the hacking of I-Chat, the search for home-address-exposing server payments, the trawling of Facebook for a list of students from Ignatius High. There had been advances (cracking the I-Chat webmaster's password without detection) and failures (coming up short on a positive ID), but before the mission could be accomplished the rage had faded for most and different thrills stole the hardcore troll's charges. One troll abandoned the attack on I-Chat to help hack an epilepsy support forum and replace the home page with seizure-inducing GIFs. Another hijacked the Facebook account of a Pentecostal pastor and updated the pastor's status: "Really feeling today that God's full of it." The troll screencapped the replies and posted them for /b/'s enjoyment. Another troll edited a video for Britney Spears's "... Baby One More Time" from footage posted by Juba the Baghdad Sniper documenting the surprising, instant deaths of all the American soldiers he cut down. The troll flooded Army Reserve forums with his creation.

Why troll? Why the fuck troll? Who asks this? For their protection, we can't say for sure. But the answers to this anonymously asked question are legion. It's bodily. That's one answer. They do it for the lulz. Schadenfreude on steroids is what these hackers on steroids are after. Lulz is the corruption of lol, the "beyond the pleasure principle" of lol: when lol's innocent and milquetoast and white Mickey Mouse gloves run through the internet hate machine to become the seething fur of the massive packs of rats that spread the bubonic plague.

To the authorities, for who there is never a single fresh thing blooming under the sun, trolls are old news. According to the cops and the twenty-four-hour news feed, trolls do it because this is what delinquents do in the twenty-first century. Another authority, the professor, will stand at the podium in a sparsely attended session at the Art in the Internet Age conference, delivering a paper titled "'The World Would Be a Better Place Without You': 4chan and the Transformation of the Satirical Mode," in which he argues trolls are satirists. This is what happens to satire when beings are so integrated into so many social symbols and global networks and interconnecting technologies. Satirists used to caricature a face by distorting its features in ink on paper. Today the self is thoroughly fused with these manipulable bits, sites and codes; and the troll is a caricaturist whose distortions destroy the very life assimilated into these social media profiles, digital images, credit card accounts and so on, ad infinitum.

The movie producer and screenwriter, planning to make the next big thing, quarrel over the historical significance of the troll. They agree on the figure central to every great American film, whether *The Godfather* or *Modern Times*, or even the mildly okay, like *Natural Born Killers*: the lone wolf virtuoso who breaks free from the limiting, rigid system. That is the key. Part hero, part demon, this guy goes rogue and harvests whatever he needs to survive – whether money, hilarity or lives. But who, in the movie they want to make, is this lone wolf? For the producer, there's no question: it's the trolls. Yet no matter what piece of evidence he presents, the screenwriter refuses to stray from his understanding of trolls as holdovers from a quainter, human-centred age. For the screenwriter, if their movie is to be true to their times, then it has to be the story of the system itself breaking free from us. The Luddite terrorist cell, which has successfully maimed four North American scientists with letter bombs, would, if privy to this conversation, agree with the screenwriter. The trolls are a sign, a symbolic goop that foretells the grey goop to which reality will be reduced if the nanotech Armageddon is not stopped.

"But aren't trolls just parasites festering around the asshole of the internet?" protests the armchair expert, sick of all the random talk, but who quickly grows meek when we turn in his direction. "I mean," he continues, stammering, "isn't this just basic goddamned, um, science, er, um, I mean, physiology. Everything needs an asshole, right? Because everything makes shit. People. Industries. Political parties. Birds. The internet."

"And he means *s-h-i-t* shit, the foulest fucking bowl-staining deuce that's ever been laid," adds one of the many sources who wish to remain anonymous. "These trolls'll make a laugh-riot running meme of a pedo caught raping little boys in Cambodia or some such whatchamafuck, calling him 'Swirlface' because all the bozo did to hide his identity in the images he made public was to digitally swirl his face (and all interlol had to do to nab him was unswirl his swirled visage)."

"That's nothing, trolls'll pretend to be a thirteen-year-old girl to trick a pedo into sending them images of his dick, to wax poetical about all the naughty things he wants to do to the imaginary girl's naughty nubile bits, and then they'll post his cock and rotten longings for all to find glee in seeing."

"That's nothing, they'll hack a real thirteen-year-old girl's email account and threaten to share all the shit she's been talking about her friends unless she shows them her tits live via webcam."

"That's nothing, they'll ..."

"That's nothing, trolls ..."

"That's nothing ..."

"That's nothing ..."

"That's nothing ..."

For the hardcore troll, it's all nothing. Though when he first visited /b/, it had something to do with something, something about the progeny of suburbia, of privilege, needing to be tourists of the truth of their times, to undertake a quest to contact what was real at the edge, to pioneer the frontiers of image and word bordered off by the mainstream: the women burned alive as witches in an east African village, the Muslim girl who loved the wrong man swarmed by a crowd that finally dispersed when a cinder block split open her love-filled skull, the episode of *The Great White Racist* in which he tricked illegal Mexican workers into deportation, the Black supremacist who demanded to a roomful of applause that all white men be castrated and all white women raped, the eight-year-old who overdosed on heroin right before the lens his young friends fixed on him, staring into those eyes that focused, then drifted, then focused, then drifted, then finally let go.

When the hardcore troll was a boy, his mom had read him a story about God putting burrs in the guts of babies curled inside their mommies' stomachs. It happened to all children before they were born. That burr remained still and unfelt, the story went, until you did something wrong or witnessed something unjust. It was then it materialized, pricking you. The clips and images the hardcore troll sought put the burr to work: the scatological feast of "2 Girls, 1 Cup"; "1 Guy, 1 Cup" with its flow of blood after the glass cracks inside the man's anal cavity; "3 Guys, 1 Hammer" with the Russian boys on the killing spree they documented blow by blow. He wanted them to grind round his burr's points, to kill its touch in the face of the total lack of good, the relentless catalogue of crap, which confirmed again and again the inevitable absence of anything miraculous or just.

The hardcore troll takes over I-Chat while the sixteen-year-old girl is in the tub. The sixteen-year-old girl's prosthesis is submerged in the water when, unbeknownst to her, the hardcore troll's email arrives in her inbox. The supervillain attack she had rendered in black and silver ink dissolves, turning the tepid water a faint, staining purple. The water drains and she stays in the tub while the shower washes the remaining suds and colour away. The subject line of the hardcore troll's email reads: "To One of the Cancers That Is Killing the Web." The email address he sends the message from is: the.internet.is.serious.biznass@gmail.com.

The body of the email is composed of a single blue link.

"Click me," it insists.

The sixteen-year-old girl, finally reading the message, obliges.

I-Chat opens in a new window.

The screen fills with her contact information and her smiling face.

The hardcore troll's assault constricts her limbs and thoughts and emotions and hopes with the chains of being seen, webs her in the pain of being transformed into a piece of spreadable, manipulable news. Her attacker hasn't simply stolen I-Chat. He has directed it against her, in his words, "@ full fucking force." The I-Chatterers she nurtured attack swiftly. Her cellphone chimes without ceasing. The landline joins in. Her mom pounds on the door, demanding to know why the phone is ringing off the hook with prank calls about something called a "lollercaust." I-Chat fills with new, original content: the sixteen-year-old girl's class photo, complete with yellow cartoon stars shopped over her eyes and the words "Future Plans: Internet Superstar"; her face shopped onto the head of the Virgin Mary; her face warped into the shape of something straight out of hell; a motivational poster that reads, "The Internet / It's Serious Business"; an image of her without her prosthesis, leaning against a locker and holding up a sign that asks, "How does I find leg?"

It makes her feel like the criminals she learned about in tenth grade history. A whole bunch of centuries ago people were punished with the wax figure of a skeleton. They were sentenced to stare at it, chained, enclosed in a room. They had to watch it watch them, or watch it peer past them into itself, its fellow skeleton trapped in skin. Her history teacher had shown a painting in one of his PowerPoint lessons. Those eyeless eyes asking, "How much longer before you can come out and decay?" She doesn't remember which crimes earned that punishment. What has she done wrong? It is the same punishment, forced to scroll down I-Chat's ever-stretching thread, sentenced to stare, F5 refreshing the page, unveiling the new material.

This is all there is to do: F5, F5, F5, F5, F5. She's doomed to scroll through that haunted virtual castle, each click spurring a new terror, the monsters all made of her by the monsters at the controls of the computers she cannot see. All those who had been attacked by others on I-Chat, all who had done the attacking and were ready to repent, all those who had lurked, spying, never typing a word, go at her online – her face, feelings, body, history and reputation. She sees herself as the princess in an untold fairy tale, trapped in a cell whose walls are made of the most horrible distorting mirrors. Someone posts an image in which her prosthesis has been replaced by the body mangled on the tracks, and the "me, me, me" she reels in alone is broken by her arrangement with this thing, this former person. This is one of her people. No, it's the other way around. She is one of its people, its subjects. She serves this king. Who was it before it became so regal? How did it know this was the way to ascend a throne? If what this thing once was could see itself now, would it go back in time and do otherwise? Would it, like her, wish only to hit F5, F5, F5?

The sixteen-year-old girl's questions about the body mangled on the tracks will, in different ways, be asked by others, along with many, many more questions. Most of them will be answered, making public what the man mangled on the tracks had hoped would remain unknown, his former name and former address, his employment history, recreational memberships and not-quite-completed certificates. An ex-girlfriend will tell reporters how his criminal record was bullshit because the guy he had been convicted of crippling had assaulted her. The relative to say more than "no comment," a nephew from out west, will describe the man as a "one step forward, two steps back kind of guy."

What will remain anonymous forever, though, was what the man on the tracks considered his final act. Not his death. Dropping forty feet from the bridge had been the final ripple of a stone cast years ago. His final act had happened the night before, at the house where The Nameless had spent their last days. He had gone to the basement to visit with the former junior hockey star but found the workroom empty. The two explosive belts sat on the bench, ready to go, the kid's distinguished with his old hockey number, seventy-seven, markered onto the canvas. After calling the kid's name once more and receiving no reply, the man had sabotaged the trigger. While the rest of them died – the guy fell to the tracks, the broker sprinted across the baseball field and blew himself up, and others slit throats and wrists, broke craniums open with triggered shells – the former junior hockey star would, rightfully, survive, would stand above the thriving city, shocked himself as he had intended to shock others, with no idea who had saved him, this act of love to remain forever unknown.

But shock doesn't work the way the man mangled on the tracks had imagined it in the basement. In his fantasy, he'd gotten the intensity of the surprise right – the kid realizing his explosives had been sabotaged. What the man had failed to imagine was how destructive this revelation could be. He didn't see the vast trail of ruins that could pile up behind the kid or the yawning void that could open in place of the days ahead. He didn't see the jolts could keep coming, like waves, capsizing the kid every time he righted the dinghy.

Just look at the budding star, hours earlier, when the accident happened.

First, there is the shock of what she sees. Then, there is the shock of the floor of the cab against her body when the train brakes. The victim preserved perfectly in her memory of that fall comes right at her again and again and seeing that fall repeat in her mind she flinches on the floor she has fallen to. When she calls in the Code 000, there is the shock of the dispatcher explaining there will be a major delay in assistance due to a pair of earlier transit crises and word that emergency services of all stripes are being called to violent scenes across the city. There is the shock of the commuters' response, many of who continue to complain about the inconvenience, even after she explains she hit someone. There is the shock of the commuters shouting, "There's somebody back there" with the body – and when she runs through the evacuated train and jumps to the tracks in the rear, there is the shock of what she sees: a lithe teen leaning over the remains, his arm pointed at the tracks like a painter measuring the proportions of his subject with his thumb. The teen does not look up at her or lift his arm, even as the budding star shouts for him to stop, and then comes the shock of his reply.

It isn't a voice that answers.

It's a single flash of light.

A cellphone camera.

The shooter takes off.

She pursues him down the tracks, shouting at him to delete that picture right now. She chases him over the fence, through the brush of the park to the backyard where she loses him. She keeps up her pursuit, though, because there is no other way to end that image. She is slowed by the shock of what she saw, barely a glance as she passed. It remains clear in her mind. Where the teen had stood with his cellphone there had been no human left at all. Only colours, dulled in the faint light cast from the rear of the train, but still colours she had never considered belonging to a body. It was the outcome of unsociable skins forced to mingle. All the outsides and insides swirled into pulp. She stops running, braces herself against a lamppost and vomits. The body as vomit. She has made someone's body into vomit. She gets sick again.

Why would the teen have taken that picture?

Why would he dishonour a body in that way?

A Citytv news van whizzes past.

The budding star starts back for her train, sprinting again, called by the body, needing to stop any further desecrations, hoping to show this life, lost, the respect it deserves. Without breaking stride, she pulls off her jacket and holds it open, wondering if it will be big enough. Maybe one of the lingering commuters will share their jacket to help her free this body from being witnessed, to grant it peace from eyes and light.

The news van, though, is speeding off to cover a different suicide, her collision not spectacular enough to register. The sheer volume of the suicides fills the Twitterverse and website headlines and regular-scheduled-program-interrupting newsbreaks. Then the suicides are overtaken by a surprising update. Contradicting earlier reports, one of the suicide victims has survived, though he remains in critical condition. The police refuse to confirm anything, but a number of people who watch the suicide attempt online identify the man as a former junior hockey star, and, to support their conviction, they provide links in the comment section to various hockey-related websites. In the footage of his death, the kid sprints across the baseball diamond beside another man. Some commenters argue the kid is pursuing the man, trying to stop him from setting off the explosive that kills the man and severely injures the kid. The witnesses interviewed after the game set the record straight. The man with the bomb and the former junior hockey star had been sitting together in the front row, holding hands or embracing through the first seven innings. There had been a long kiss, too, right before they took off together onto the field.

What do you think the other anons think of this – the thus far unnamed, and yet the most advanced and experienced and expert of them all? What do the "old" think, the "aged," as some say, or, in the words of others, "all those useless decrepit fucks"? What do they make of the news of the suicides?

Here they are, eleven of the millions, arranged around a forty-inch flat screen in the entertainment room of St. Anthony House. The news of the rash of suicides, potentially a cult-initiated incident, interrupts an episode of a police procedural about a drug-addicted officer. The urgent notes of the newsbreak's theme demand the unwavering attention of anyone within sensory range. But these, remember, are the members of a century-long generation that, in the history of every beast and being, has seen more change, for better and for worse, more promise, failed and realized, than any generation before. If creatures were catalogued by the characteristics and qualities of their time, then their generation would be distinguished as a species at once new, rare and nearly extinct. So don't blame them for not being shocked by what the anchorman describes as the shocking tragedy of these suicides, or for not feeling the longing the anchorman attributes to his audience: the need to receive more details as they emerge.

Not every one of these anonymous residents is "old." There's the former carpenter-by-day-musician-by-night who, by the age of forty-four, had guzzled alcohol to such excess he could no longer make new memories. He glances up at the television screen and blurts, "I worked with that guy," even though he never did. The next morning, as he does every morning, the former carpenter will rise for a condo job completed over a decade ago, and when he plays his next weekly gig at St. Anthony, the nurses, as they always do, will tell him which song to play next so he doesn't sing, again and again, the song he knows is best for opening. There is also the thirtysomething whose eyes loll, wet and blank, in the television screen's direction. A few years back, she drank battery acid, destroying her insides, damaging her brain and banishing her to a monosyllabic, semi-vegetative state – though her ex-husband acts otherwise, sharing the day-to-day minutiae when he visits her with the boys.

For most of the residents, the shift from the TV show to the news is a fleeting distraction. The childless octogenarian who had dedicated much of her life to being the best aunt she could turns from the screen and takes up her never-ending game of solitaire with cards no one else can see, her hand carefully dusting across nothing to turn nothing over, to lift nothing in front of her face for careful consideration, to place nothing atop an ordered pile of nothing. The long-retired rancher who has not had a visitor in years toes away from the entertainment room in his wheelchair and creeps through the halls of the home, as he is apt to do, pulling weakly at his seat belt and demanding to know who trapped him in this goddamned machine. How the hell do you get out of this thing? Why the hell won't they let him go?

Only the seventy-seven-year-old who refuses to wear anything other than her blue nightie is disturbed by the intrusion of the news. She shoots out of her recliner for the third time that night and dashes to the television to change the channel. She needs to watch *The Andy Griffith Show*, and it is almost finished, she just knows it. A warm-voiced man who might be her uncle Bill promises to do what he can and helps her back to her chair. He gives her a pill to silence that urging part of her, the part that says go watch *Andy Griffith*, stilling, too, her tapping foot, her shaking fingers, as she watches the face of the young man who, according to the anchor, is the lone survivor of what appears to be a mass suicide, though the young man remains in critical condition.

The face of the lone survivor passes into the pattern of a wide receiver's route, passes into the pattern of a vehicle, all-purpose and massive, tearing through the mucky and daunting terrain of a morning forest. A dissipating guitar riff gives way to a voiced opinion on the current state of affairs, which gives way to an argument over a crime scene's contents, which gives way to the special report of an entertainment news magazine. The host stands on a brightly lit and geometrically attuned set; a wall-sized screen behind her displays the face of two young Black men, twins, beneath the words *The Quest*.

"Welcome back," she says, flashing a welcoming smile at a new camera angle. "Now, as promised, I want to give you exclusive details about the major reality TV event of 2011: *The Quest*."

The stars of the show are eighteen-year-old twins, she explains, who were taken from their native Rwanda as babies and brought to live in the USA. They have grown up learning nothing about their culture and knowing nothing about their biological parents. To undo that injustice, the twins are being sent with a group of twenty-four paired contestants from all walks of life. While learning with the boys about their Tutsi heritage, the contestants will compete in elimination challenges designed to lead the winning team to find the twins' long-lost parents.

"Though the network has not released any official figures," the host exclaims, "industry insiders have speculated the twins, their family and the winning contestants of *The Quest* will split more than five million dollars in cash and prizes."

Turning again to the original camera angle, the host speaks in a hushed tone about the next exclusive insider look: the world premiere of *The Quest*'s promotional footage. More footage will appear on upcoming episodes. She offers in awe the scoop that this footage is not rehearsed and is not the work of a trained network crew. Every episode of *The Quest* will include the segment "Real Rwanda," the footage captured with one hundred percent authenticity by local Rwandans, free to film as they pleased, with cameras the network generously provided.

The footage begins with a dirt street lined with single-storey shanties, the sun beyond setting, feet walking bare through the dirt. A group of men soiled with work address the camera with serious and sincere stares. Next, a different dirt street brightens with a group of children rambling playfully away. One points at the camera, turns to his friends laughing and then turns back to the camera, his mouth smiling as wide as a world cracked in two. In different scenes, others who do not notice the camera keep at what they keep at: herding chickens through a rusted wire fence, sitting on a stool and tossing stones at something beyond the range of the lens. A woman in close-up, surrounded by lightly clothed and excited bodies, braces a baby gasping from between the legs of another woman. A man jumps from high foliage, past a waterfall and into the river pooling brown below. When he jumps, all there is for a moment is sky.

As the seventy-seven-year-old in the blue nightie nods off, the former junior hockey star enters his third hour of surgery. The fluids and people and monitors and tools are so dedicated to saving his life they become one unnameable being, and he is so open to their efforts he, too, is one with what they've become. Think of the first time wood was driven into earth to make shelter. It's that kind of fantastical union. What happens as he dies? Imagine a television watching only its own static flow. Imagine a camera looking in upon and filming the blank infinity of its famous stare. This is what happens. With all that pain and sensation taken away by the anaesthetic, he hears no hearing, and sees no seeing, and he senses nothing of how it feels to be something that senses and feels. In that moment's finality, in its ridiculousness, in that instant which, from the perspective of the particulars of everything he had been and believed could not help but emerge as impossible, there is no thought, no content or consequence, only the most anonymous form of life as life's last anonymous form, one breath away from disappearing for good.

FORT MAC IS BOOMING

BRANDY PRIDDLE DIDN'T WANT ME TO HAVE NOTHING to do with it. "You're a loser, Zwick," she said, and she sure as shit didn't need any of that rubbing off on the little guy in her belly, the one she referred to as *her* son. This was back in 2005, so I was only twenty, too young to be a loser as far as I saw it. If life was a game, I'd barely left the bench long enough to break a sweat. One of the waitresses at the restaurant where I washed dishes had heard from a friend that I'd knocked up Brandy. That's how I got the news. I tried to play it cool, giving a sly shoulder shrug in reply, my eyes squinting over an effortless smirk, which for some reason made the waitress burst out laughing. I took off to do a garbage run, smoking like a chimney and texting friend after friend in search of Brandy's number. I called her and she confirmed the worst and she started calling me a loser in every way possible. If we were going to talk about losers, I said, then we should say a few words about the heifer who sells pills while waiting tables at that shithole on the east end. I wondered if that heifer's manager would like to know more about that. Brandy screeched like someone had squished those fat cheeks of hers between two hot irons. I didn't want nothing to do with a kid born into that septic tank she called a family. I told her so and hung up.

I had been between jobs when I wheeled up Brandy at The Club, the after-hours place the Hells Angels ran on South Hill. I had just been fired from the truck wash, where I was low man on the totem and always got stuck pressure washing cow and pig shit out of the back of those double-decker trailers. I had decided to set out for Fort Mac to surprise my brother who worked a crew that built roads for hauling around all that oil-soaked sand. My brother had sent an email to a bunch of his buddies from back home and included me on the list. He said it was booming. All the money, drugs and pussy you could ever need. Fort Mac was the paradise terrorists thought they were heading to when they blew themselves to high heaven. That was why I had slept with Brandy in the first place. I didn't want to land in Fort Mac a virgin. I was drunk as balls and it was a real struggle not to snicker at all the random shit that kept popping into my head. Like when I finally yanked her bra off and saw she had these weird, mesa-shaped tits. The whole time we were doing it those puppies stood stout and firm on the roiling desert of her pink rolls. I couldn't handle her face, either. All I could think was that if she shaved her hair off and squeezed her eyes tight shut, her head would look like a plucked, decapitated chicken.

I never made it to Fort Mac. My brother ended up getting some sort of a mental illness and killing himself. My mom called and told me so. That was the first time we'd talked since I'd left the farm for Moose Jaw. She didn't say how he did it. I didn't ask. I never saw my son after he was born, either. At the start of the summer, when I first heard Brandy had had him, I texted her to see if he'd come out all right. A few weeks later, Brandy's two older brothers and a cousin kicked the living shit out of me in front of The Royal. I'm not sure if they did it because they thought I was planning to get involved in the kid's life or if they thought I was being a deadbeat and needed to cough up dough. Their pleasantries were limited to "fucking piece of shit" and the grunts that punctuated each punch, stomp, slap and kick. The beating dulled my sense of what was going on outside me. There was just this old-timey cop inside my head saying things like "Move along, Zwick," and, "Nothing to see here," and "You've got to turn your life around." The blow that knocked me out landed right after I heard my voice sputter through my own blood and broken teeth, "Your sister's pussy tasted like a dead dog's ass."

* * *

Out of the hospital, I knew if I was going to make a clean start, I needed to find a real career. Smitty's was decent enough and, like the old dishwasher saying goes, which I had made up and kept to myself, "The Empire that spans a thousand miles begins with a single sud." Rob, the kitchen manager, was the real highlight of that gig. He didn't let the cooks or servers call me Zwick the Prick or Dish Pig, the Dish Pig nickname falling to the guy who worked dinner shifts. Rob liked me because I said "please," "thanks" and "yes, sir," and I was willing to stay after I'd clocked out to do odd jobs like help replace the deep fryer or rearrange the walk-in freezer. Rob was also impressed that with a broken wrist and two cracked ribs I still worked faster than the Dish Pig. Rob said he could talk to his sister-in-law, who was a cop, about the Priddle boys, but I said I just wanted to let the past be the past. The truth was, I had amassed a shit ton of parking tickets when I thought I was moving to Fort Mac and I didn't need any bullshit from the law.

Dennis Sentes, the founder and owner of Dennistiny Sales Saskatchewan, was my ticket to finally taking my life to the next level. The ad in the back of the *Moose Jaw Times Herald* said it all: "Highly Motivated Salespeople Wanted for Revolutionary Business." Dennis was the real deal. He had a suit, that messy haircut all the hockey players sported and a van with the Dennistiny logo painted on both sides: a sun with a cartoon of Dennis's face either sinking behind or rising out of a prairie horizon. To top it all off, Dennis was a nice guy. During the interview, when I told him the Priddle brothers were the reason I looked half-zombie, he said all I had to do was give him the thumbs-up and he would have his lawyer sue those inbreds black and blue.

I had moved to Moose Jaw to study at SIAST and the Business Marketing course was the one I gave two shits about during the only term I took before dropping out. So I could see right away Dennis had come up with a truly one-of-a-kind strategy. Mobility and adaptability, he said, were the keys to surviving the twenty-first century. Why tie yourself down to a store with all the taxes and rent? And did anyone really trust online sellers? We beat both by selling directly to our customers, face to face in the parking lot at the Town 'n' Country Mall, or in the Staples' parking lot, or on Main Street sidewalks, though the store owners downtown were usually quick to the call the cops. Depending on how Dennis was feeling about the markets, we would fill our arms and duffel bags with pots and pans, or stuffed animals and battery-operated robots, or garden tools and ornaments, and hit the pavement. That's why I had to cut my hair, which I had not cut since leaving home. I scared the living shit out of these ladies leaving Walmart. When they saw me coming with arms full of knives, my face swollen and stitched from the beating, and my hair hanging past my shoulders, they screamed and the old one spun around and ran smack into the sliding door that had shut behind her. I got my hair cut like Dennis. He told me which product to buy so when I messed up the front it would hold just right.

Pulling in two paycheques, I was finally able to move out of my basement apartment and ask the love of my life, Laurie Brierly, to move into a one bedroom with me. Dennis gave me a deal on Dennistiny pots and pans for a housewarming present. I'd met Laurie at Blockbuster, where she was a shift supervisor, earlier that year, right after I learned about Brandy being knocked up. I'd had a bit of a mishap in her store. Some mouth-breathing new guy said I couldn't rent without photo ID, which was bullshit considering I probably paid their energy bill with all the money I spent. I did something stupid like tip over a candy stand or stomp open a two-litre pop or both. Instead of demanding I get the hell out of her store and never come back, Laurie stopped the mouth-breather from calling the cops and asked me if I wanted to talk. She gave me the smile I had seen her give me every time she handed me my rentals. I could tell it was meant to be a sweet smile, but some sort of feeling inside her stopped it from fully coming to life, like this pain knotted her lips and cheeks in strands of invisible fish wire. I returned her smile. I suppose my smile was as sweet as the pain inside me allowed. I'd never really looked in a mirror to check.

When Laurie got off work that night, we went down the block to Tim's and talked until 4:00 a.m. If I hadn't had a breakfast shift at Smitty's, I bet we could have talked until 4:00 a.m. the next morning. Laurie had a real head on her shoulders. She was nothing like Brandy, whose life goal, as far as I could tell, consisted of getting fat, getting high and pushing pills. I liked to get as fucked up as the next guy, but there was more to life than blades and beers and lines. Brandy was so far gone that, according to one of the cooks at Smitty's, she had intentionally gotten knocked up the night I banged her because she had heard the courts wouldn't send you to jail for dealing drugs if you were a woman and had a little kid. Laurie, rather than buying into any meth-invented hocus-pocus, had a real plan. She wasn't just into movies. Her favourite TV show was *CSI* and it had inspired her to pursue a career in forensic science, which was why she was upgrading her high school maths and saving some dough by living with her parents. I told her everything about Brandy, the baby, my brother doing himself in. After the first time Laurie and I did it, I held her close and she said that one day she wanted to have a baby. That sounded really good, and I said so.

* * *

Back in those days, my life was like a wild bronco. No matter how hard I fought to wrangle him, that sucker always bucked free. There was no taming it. My choice was: beat the creature to death or let it run wild. Everything I worked so hard to turn around eventually got turned back around on me. It started in September when Dennis gathered me and the rest of the sales crew together in the Civic Centre parking lot and said Moose Jaw was drying up. Dennistiny Sales would be shifting its innovative retail operations to Regina. I quit my job washing dishes to take the newly created assistant sales director position with Dennistiny. Rob was so pissed at me for not giving him two weeks' notice he made up some shit about Dennis hightailing it out of town because he had been told by the cops to leave or face a judge.

The commute to Regina and back five days a week got worse when the rest of the Moose Jaw sales crew quit, forcing me to ride the Greyhound. Then some Superstore-hired goons smashed up the Dennistiny Sales van and we had to hit the road every day. Dennis, myself and the Einsiedler brothers from North Battleford, who'd signed up with us in Regina, travelled across southern Saskatchewan, from town to city to town, Monday through Friday, and I ended up blowing my wages on takeout, hotels, whisky, gas for the van, uppers the Einsiedlers scored and the Greyhound bus I caught home late Friday night and then back out on Sunday to Estevan or Piapot or Liberty or wherever it was we were hawking our wares next.

The Einsiedler brothers bowed out of Dennistiny in Saskatoon, taking with them our wallets and six boxes of no-stick cookware. For dinner that night, Dennis and I split an All-American Slam at Denny's, paying for it with change we found in the glove compartment. Dennis parked the van behind a place called Absolute Drywall after the Travelodge security chased us out of their parking lot. Without a word, we both pretended to sleep, neither of us stirring when we heard a group of howling, drunken teens stop outside the van and spray it up. They X'd out one of the Dennistiny suns. They added a stick man's body to the other and a massive, van-long cock.

I managed to get back on at Smitty's washing dishes, but the hours were part-time and Rob, still pissed at me for quitting, didn't stop the cooks and servers from calling me Dish Pig Part 2 or the Return of Zwick the Dick. Plus, I had nothing to do in my spare time but drink, so I missed the odd shift and wasn't as quick with my "pleases" and "yes, sirs." Laurie's grandfather had been a vile drunk. She'd met him once, when she was five, and all she remembered was him trying to put a cigarette out on her forehead for making too much noise when she turned the pages of her comic book. I swore I'd quit drinking, didn't, but when Laurie dumped what I'd thought had been my secret stash down the sink I didn't say a word. I hadn't given her my half of the rent in three months.

Pot ended up being our compromise. She liked how it increased her creative thinking, which she said was the most important skill for forensic scientists. She'd take another toke and rattle off a bunch of examples from *CSI* that didn't make any sense to me. She was one of those people dope made laugh and laugh and laugh. We'd barely make it through the opening credits of a movie before she'd have to pause the flick to go pee and catch her breath. Pot just made me paranoid as hell, but it was better than nothing. The veins that ran along the surface of my body would pulse, and the corners of my eyes, nose and mouth would twitch, and it would all happen in such a way I found it impossible to believe some evil genius did not have a remote control programmed to turn my body against me.

This one time I ate shrooms and smoked up and my brother's ghost visited me and said that if I did not move to Fort Mac he was going to kill me.

"It's booming," he said.

I could see him right there, on the other side of the window, covered in frost and floating two storeys off the ground.

"That's your reflection," Laurie kept saying, which might have explained what I was seeing but did nothing to account for his voice booming, "Move!"

Laurie disappeared into the bedroom and returned with a mickey of gin, the one soldier she had saved from my slaughtered secret stash. She had kept the gin for when I was good, but an emergency called it into action. Alcohol, she had heard, could cut into a psychedelic high and help temper mad hallucinations. Sitting underneath the kitchen table, so I would quit hustling back to the window to see if my brother was about to smash through the glass, we passed the bottle back and forth, like a pair of caged big cats pacing back and forth over the same argument. Fort Mac was just a bunch of oil pigs and prostitutes, Laurie would plead for me to see, and I would counter that my brother said we were going to make a killing.

Laurie finally gave up.

"Fine, you want to move to Fort Mac?" she shouted. "We'll move to Fort Mac. But I hope you know I won't let you do nothing alone. Not even head to 7-Eleven. My sister said they got hookers hanging out there waiting to suck men off for the price of a Slurpee."

"Why would they do that for a Slurpee?"

"They do it for drugs, stupid. I mean it costs the same as a Slurpee."

Laurie collapsed into the mangled sprawl, limbs awry, of one of the bodies from her shows, the final pose a corpse strikes before being tape-outlined by the police. The gin had worked. My brother was gone. I kissed Laurie's tears away. I pulled her clothes away. We went from being so divided to being one when she welcomed me inside.

She pulled my head close to hers and panted in my ear, "I want this forever, Zwick. Us."

"Forever," I panted back in her ear. "Me, too."

And I repeated that longing, "Forever," into her ear. I repeated it again and again and again as the pleasure migrated gradually from our loins to our buttocks to our stomachs and legs and chests and necks and minds, the ecstasy billowing outward like the debris storm of a demolished building played in slow mo.

"Zwick!" Laurie snapped, stilling me with a sharp squeeze on the shoulders. "Stop saying that word!"

"Forever?"

"No. 'Booming.' You keep saying, booming, booming, booming, booming."

Laurie finally left me a few days before Christmas. My mom called while I was at work. This had come as a real surprise to Laurie, considering I'd told her my parents were dead. She didn't wait for me to return home to leave. I called and texted non-stop. She never picked up or replied, though she did move back in with me two days later. I had left a message saying the next thing she would hear was I had gone the way of my brother, like we were both dodos. Brushing her fingers through my close-cropped hair while I wept against her thighs, she made me promise never to hurt myself or lie to her again. She made me promise to get back in touch with my mom.

"She seems like a good woman," Laurie said.

The surface of the ocean seems good, too, until you're tossed into a writhing school of double-toothed sharks, oil-squirting squids and whales as wild as two PCP-addled football teams. That's what I wanted to say. I didn't. I promised to call my mom in the New Year.

Laurie and I spent Christmas with her parents. Things started out fine. Laurie gave me a bunch of previously viewed DVDs and I made everyone a big breakfast with eggs, bacon and waffle mix only Laurie knew I'd swiped from Smitty's. That's when Laurie's mom blew it. She let it slip that Laurie had not stayed with them after she threw a fit and left me. It turned out she had crashed on the couch at her new manager's place. I wasn't in a position to do anything but slap on a smile as wide as a stuck hyena's, polish off the bottle of Crown we'd bought Laurie's dad for Christmas and stew as the room dissolved into a cloud of barely perceptible grime until the voice of Laurie's dad confirmed my expulsion with the immortal blessing, "Get the fuck out of my house."

* * *

I stayed with the Dish Pig. His real name was Tyler, but he preferred to be called Dish Pig. He said his nickname made him feel like an outlaw or a professional wrestler. As far as that went, I didn't mind being called Zwick the Dick either. The Dish Pig's mom rented the main floor of one of these old four-storey beauties Moose Jaw's bankers and retired ranchers and mayors might have owned in the old days, but that had since been butchered with walls and side entrances to convert one home into eight separate apartments. I slept when the Dish Pig was at work, he slept when I was at work, and we drank our faces off at night, which suited his mom just fine because she worked graveyards at Tim's. I never called Laurie. I was so finished with her that I didn't bother replying when she texted to arrange a time for me to pick up my stuff. If she wanted a fresh start with her new manager, she could have it.

It turned out the Dish Pig had a lot of talents. He did incredible impersonations of cartoon characters – Mickey Mouse, Marge Simpson, Buzz Lightyear – which were pop-a-colon hilarious because he would say the filthiest things. He was also a world-class player at *Call of Duty* for the Xbox. I'd never had a video game console growing up, so the multi-button controller made about as much sense to me as the insides of a dissected rhino. I was just happy watching a master at work. He'd blast to smithereens the asses of players from across the globe, the whole time trash-talking his opponents in the voices of SpongeBob SquarePants or Daffy Duck. Our second-biggest pastime was talking shit about the losers at work, which made washing dishes at least a quarter bearable because I was always on the lookout to add to our catalogue of stupidity. The odd night we went to bed at the same time we'd talk about the different things we'd do to the different waitresses. The Dish Pig was good at that, too, imagining the dirty details. I'd reach my hand under my blanket and jerk off as quiet as I could and pretend what he was saying was happening to me. If I listened really hard, I thought I could hear him doing the exact same thing.

January kicked off with a city-shuttering blizzard, and we both got the whole day off. This was not the best timing. The Dish Pig's impersonations were getting pretty old by that point and the only person I wanted to bitch about was him. He needed to do something with his life, and I told him so. Without looking away from the soldier-filled screen, he told me if I tried to be his daddy then the something I could do with my life was suck his big fat wang. All I knew, I said to him, was I was heading to Fort Mac, while it was still booming. He didn't know about my brother doing himself in, so I said my brother was going to hook me up with prime employment, which was partly true because I knew the name of the company my brother had worked for from the picture of him grinning beside a T. Rex–sized tire. I told the Dish Pig I just needed to give my brother the word and he would get me a job faster than the devil can say, "Sin." Old news, was the Dish Pig's reply. Not only Fort Mac, but the whole fucking continent. He said I might as well try making babies with a ninety-year-old whore who's been fist-fucked with a catcher's mitt. China was the next big thing. That was why he had mastered these video games. He had heard the Chinese were charting the scores on games like *Call of Duty* with the idea of recruiting the top ranked players to control the robot army they were building to invade North America. I told him he sounded like he had a bit of mental illness.

"You better start practising, Zwick," he said, glaring at me, "or you'll be the first on my list."

He made a gun of his hand and pointed it at me. His mouth produced a sound when he fired, I could tell by how his lips moved, but I couldn't hear it over the roar of the game.

I went to the front room and sat on the couch by the window. The blizzard was so thick the tree in the yard could have been the fleshless arm of a withered giant reaching out from its grave. I watched the storm from late morning through the afternoon and into the night, finishing the case of Canadian I'd cracked at breakfast, the flurries still making the street look like it was getting terrible reception. More than anything, I wanted to venture out into that storm and be gone from there. I wanted to go back to Laurie. I wanted to walk back to our apartment and apologize for everything, and to ask her to apologize for everything too, or even just one thing each. She didn't even have to say what, just "I'm sorry," and we could start again, like the apology would give birth to us, would be our mom and dad, and we its children, new and knowing nothing and ready to begin.

I passed out thinking that and woke wanting the same. Not even a real miracle of a headache could stop me from calling her. My skull was at once an earthquaking fault line and a pair of teeth being flossed with piano wire, but I still managed to leave a message saying, "I need to see you." The talk at work was the lives the storm had taken, the cars it had killed or stalled or swallowed. One couple, setting out on foot, had frozen ten metres from home. I phoned Laurie on my break. She didn't pick up. I left another message saying I had almost ventured out in the storm for her, and I asked her how she would have felt if I had frozen for her love.

The Dish Pig made extra money playing *Call of Duty* against guys around town, which he always did in person to make sure his opponents didn't use any cheats. The day after the blizzard, the Dish Pig was off, so he picked me up in his mom's car when I finished at one. I wanted to buy a bag of weed for Laurie, who had not returned any of my calls, and the guys who rented the place he was playing at were dealers. One of the guys, wearing a Fox Head Motocross hat backwards, answered the door and invited us into a room that smelled like the underside of a shit-harvested mushroom. We dropped our coats in the pile at the door.

There were already six guys gathered around the massive TV screen, the size of a semi's grill. They barely glanced away from the heavily armed Xbox avatars to say, "Hey," when the Dish Pig joined them. I bought a bag of pot off the Fox Head guy. I asked him if he wanted to smoke some with me and he led me into the kitchen.

On the table, there was a baby sleeping in a car seat, which the Fox Head guy had to nudge aside to make space to roll the joint. With nothing to say to one another, we both watched the baby sleep as we passed the joint back and forth.

"Peaceful," I finally said, the weed easing my headache and loosening me up.

"He was bawling," the Fox Head guy said, smiling for the first time, "but I gave him a little something to help him sleep."

"You're a good dad," I said, smiling back. "Start him young."

"I'm not the dad."

"Whose kid is it?"

"Brandy Priddle's."

I stared straight at the baby, feigning a look of unknowing indifference. But I was afraid to turn away, like this child was one of those spots on the periphery that if you turned slightly it disappeared.

"Is Brandy here?" I asked.

"Naw, she went out."

"Where to?"

"Fuck if I know. I'm not her dad, either."

The Fox Head guy took one last pull on the joint, dropped the roach in a half-empty beer and left to watch the match of *Call of Duty*, which I could tell from the profanities the Dish Pig shouted in the voice of Shrek had already begun. I asked where the can was, and I stood in there for as long as it would take to piss then flushed the toilet. I crept back into the living room. The war on the screen kept any of them from hearing me grab my jacket and the car keys from the Dish Pig's jacket. I crept back to the kitchen. I picked up the car seat, my son, and we escaped through the rear.

* * * .

Laurie got it, what I saw when I saw my boy in that kitchen: opportunity. The blank slate of his fat face had conjured in me an extraordinary blend of pride and fear and longing and joy. I had it in me to feed or fell millions, whatever my son wished to command. But with that vision of limitless opportunity, I had glimpsed another limitless opportunity: all the losers with their loser habits and losing ways threatening to engulf him, reaching out like the tentacle-shaped flames of a dying planet flaring on the heels of the one ship that's this close to getting away. It was like the intestines of the life that reduced most of us to shit had briefly turned translucent and I could see him up there, not chewed to pieces yet, not swallowed. Laurie held him while I packed a suitcase with the few things of mine she hadn't thrown out yet. She saw what I saw. It radiated off him like a full-body halo. I took my boy back from her so she could pack. I changed his diaper.

Laurie agreed we needed to escape to Fort Mac, and she reiterated this as she went to the kitchen. I had no idea what I would have done if she had said no. I needed Laurie to be a mother to my son and to fund our move to Fort Mac. Once we settled, she could stay home with my son, have a kid of her own, too, while I shot up the ranks in my brother's old company, crushing gravel or driving one of those big trucks like my brother. I was so broke I'd had to lift diapers and juice boxes from Shoppers.

Over the sound of banging pots, Laurie wondered if it might be smart to stop by her new manager's place. She couldn't see me from the kitchen, but I could tell she could tell by how quiet I got that I was pissed.

"There was never nothing between us," she said, still rustling with the pans in the kitchen. "He's married with kids and it was his wife's idea I stay there."

She thought it would be wise to drop in and get some quick pointers on caring for a baby, which neither of us knew anything about. It would also give her the chance to say goodbye to a few of her Blockbuster friends, who she had planned to join at her new manager's place to witness this big comet pass by the Earth, one of the manager's kids having received a telescope for Christmas.

"It could be neat for your son," she added, "not that he'll remember, of course, but it's something we could tell him he was there to see."

I thought about it as I dressed my freshly diapered boy. I thought about all I didn't know about the things a boy would want to know about, all the things I'd wanted to know about but nowhere along the line had anyone bothered to tell me. I didn't really know what a comet was, what it was made of, how it survived zipping around outer space. All that would have to come later, I decided. We needed to figure out how to make it to Fort Mac with a stolen car and what could be misconstrued as a stolen baby.

I called back to Laurie, "We're leaving right now."

I put my boy in his car seat and gave him another juice box. He looked as pleased as a king after coronation.

Laurie hurried out of the kitchen with a big sad smile, like she was coming to give me a kiss after hearing my favourite ferret had died. She stopped about a foot short, her hand reaching out to touch my face. "You didn't need to do this," she said. "You should have just come home on your own."

She glanced over my shoulder, at my boy, her face twisting in horror as she screamed, "Oh my God!"

I turned to save him.

That was when she hit me. Right in the side of my skull. The blow seemed to make my cranium split into all these different layers, like one of the fancy pastries they sell at Tim's, and each of these layers was set ablaze. I was cracked so kookily I wondered at first how I had missed that nation-shaped birthmark on my son's forehead before it finally clicked: it was a splash of my own blood.

I turned to face Laurie. She was in a crouch – partly surprised I was still standing and partly ready to strike again. She had hit me with the giant frying pan from the set Dennis had discounted for our housewarming present. The saucer lay at her feet. She held the busted handle in both hands. She had the pathetic appearance of someone playing baseball for the first time after bragging they were a home run king. I took the handle from her. I drove the busted end into her throat until it broke skin.

I didn't kill her because she hit me, or not just because she hit me. I killed her because after making me swear on my brother's grave I would never lie to her again, I saw she had been lying to me all that time. I killed her because it would have been a lie not to kill her. I felt inconsolably sorry for her when I saw her crouching there with that broken handle and realized she had tried to take me out with a frying pan. I thought: This is the one thing you know, these mysterious murders and perfect crimes, and of all the tricks of the fatal trade TV had taught you, this is the best you can come up with? A frying pan is all you've got? I felt shame bordering on disgust. She'd failed me, failed herself, with her feeble attempt at going free.

I took Laurie's bank card. The money she had saved for school would help my boy and I move to Fort Mac and leave us enough to get by for a few weeks while we figured out how to create new identities. I lugged Laurie's body to the tub and used her phone to text one of her Blockbuster friends, "Not feeling well. :(Staying home." After moving the dope I'd bought Laurie from her suitcase to mine, I packed the car, loading up my son, our suitcases and all the food from the fridge worth saving. Wanting to hightail it out of town as fast as I could, I waited to use the ATM at Belle Plaine. I played it safe and tried to withdraw three hundred bucks from Laurie's account, but the screen warned, "Insufficient Funds." I printed up the balance. "Overdraft," it read, "14.86."

I felt bad for her again, in a much different way than before, though, like I just wanted there to be one good thing for her. I wanted her ideal self to cross into our world from some other dimension, the Laurie who had half a brain and actually understood all that forensic stuff. I wanted her to find her own body, dead in the tub, and hunt me down. You better work quick, was the message I sent out to her, because my boy and I are about to hit the road and once we're rolling there won't be a soul out there, from this dimension or the rest of them, who can stop us.

* * *

This was the new world. My son and I, a regular pair of pioneers, discovered it – the mythical, elusive, unsettled realm that subsisted within this depleted nation, cutting like an ore-rich bolt through miles of useless rock. It was the people of this nation who had harvested this land. They had themselves become a land to be harvested. They were the grounds for a new community, a new source of resources and wealth, which my son and I were free to reap.

Our first few hours of exploration brought bounties. My son and I drove out to where I had grown up. I was more familiar with the territory and knew which folks went south for the winter. We hit three farms for supplies: grabbed a better set of wheels, a handgun, food and drink, including all the juice boxes and Del Monte canned fruit my boy could dream of. Fort Mac called. It yipped and howled like a pack of coyotes that we, a couple of coyotes ourselves, had strayed from. "Sun's coming up," that pack bayed. "Hurry home."

Even after the truck crashed – which I took full responsibility for, admitting to my son that if I had driven with more care, I would have slowed before striking a patch of black ice – things stayed on the up and up. One of those little eco-cars pulled over to help. It was about as suitable for those weather conditions as a plastic spoon would be for tunnelling a mountain pass, but we were in no position to choose. I left most of our new supplies in the truck, bringing my suitcase and all the diapers, juice boxes and canned fruit I could fit in the gym bag I was using as a diaper bag – once I'd packed the pistol and shells, of course.

The guy who picked us up in that world-saving car of his was a journalist. He was on his way up to Fort Mac to research a book and he offered to drive us to Cold Lake where we could find someone to tow our truck. He wasn't much older than me, say twenty-five or so, but he talked with such authority I wouldn't have been surprised if he thought he was the ghost of the ancestors of my ancestors. He used lots of big words to boast his big opinions – the kinds of ideas you'd think would take a lot of years to put together. Truth be told, his ideas were not put together as clearly as he thought. Trying to see what he was saying was like trying to peer through a metre-thick sheet of ice. I couldn't help glancing back at my son with one of those skeptical faces that says, "Can you believe this guy?" The journalist agreed Fort Mac was booming, but that was a bad thing. He went on about pollution and labour practices and coke pits and the rise of rare cancers and fugitive emissions and the evils of capitalism.

I've never been much for sharing what I think, but this guy, especially for a journalist, was so closed-minded – only seeing one side of the story, as they say. I was doing a public service trying to unbolt his eyes to another possibility. Not that I thought I had the one hundred percent correct answer, but it's important to remain open to other ways of seeing the world.

I shared some of what I had figured out about capitalism, which I'd gotten a handle on during my one semester at SIAST. It happened in a real yawner of a class on the issues facing what the professor called First Nations people, which was his word for Indians. We were having a class discussion on the meaning of the term *minority* when it hit me: the billionaire was the truest minority, the purest marginal figure. He was always excluded from us, the masses of poor, the failures and losers, the waste and the filth of the system. And to know there was nothing he could do to save us from being waste and filth, to help us become him – no language or dance or ceremony he could teach us, no dye job or surgery he could pay to have performed on us – to know he was helpless, that was the billionaire's burden.

One day, though, if things work out right, this burden will be relieved. One day, one man will own every last dollar. Man-made drones will watch over an entirely man-made world free of all men save this last one. There will be no more great wars or mass starvations or global slavery. There will be no more animals to hunt and kill one another in the wild, and no more wild to grow and die and rot. This last man will reproduce himself in a test tube, or, better, live eternally through cell regeneration. This man is the second coming. He is the bringer of the redemption of oneness. The maker of total, unbreakable world peace.

The journalist didn't think much of that, which was good, as it meant he and I gelled on at least one point: I didn't think much of what he thought, either. I let him know so with my pistol. Then I lied and said I didn't know who the baby belonged to. I didn't give two shits about the kid, and if the journalist didn't do as he was told, I would kill the baby with my bare hands right in front of him. I put on a real show, shouting so hard my face turned the purple of a beating-bruised back and spitting when I screamed. My son, playing along, bawled and bawled and bawled. The stink of the journalist's piss filled the car. I asked him not to make a habit of that. In this crew, there was only room for one member in diapers.

* * *

There was one problem, though. My son wouldn't quit bawling, and nothing could bring him peace. Not entering Fort Mac's city limits and adding our powder to the endurance of its boom. Not setting up shop in the smart hotel room the journalist, obeying my orders, rented for us. I was helpless. I bound the journalist to the toilet while my boy bawled like he had swallowed a hive of riled up bees. He wouldn't take juice or fruit, and a bath and a fresh diaper made him howl louder.

The cries of my little descendant were everything to me, and I knelt before the bed on which he shook his balled-up fists. He was like some mythical beast asking again and again the only question in the whole wide world and I alone was responsible for answering. He took on the proportions of a volcano. I lived in his looming, craggy shadow, willing to make any sacrifice to stop the molten lava from bursting out and raining down. The journalist had done everything I had asked of him. He had ditched his eco-car. He had bought us a solid used half-ton. He had given me all the cash he had. Just one more task, I told him. After this, no more. Open your mouth wide when I submerge you face first in the water-filled tub. His throat constricted under the telephone cord I roped around his neck. I showed my son what I had done for him. He remained unsatisfied.

I tried to sleep, believing my son and I so fully inhabited this new territory together, that we were bound in the same state of feeling and need. He could not sleep unless I slept, eat unless I ate or dream unless I dreamed, but my boy's bawling combined with the Red Bull and caffeine pill cocktails I'd been downing stopped me from snatching a wink.

Desperate, I grabbed the newspaper the journalist had picked up in the lobby and turned to the phone. That was the answer: until I secured a job, and truly entered the boom, my son and I remained outsiders. It was late, but this was the city of twenty-four hours of everything – work and tail. The men I reached out to for help answered, but there was nothing doing. Every extracting and refining and transporting and building company I called about the advertised positions said I needed some sort of paper or certificate or degree or experience. After two hours in Fort Mac's firing engine, I'd nearly been fully combusted and expelled. I resorted to my reserves and phoned the company my brother had worked for. The guy said I needed papers. I said I didn't really need them to build roads. I told him that's what my brother had said.

"He didn't have any papers," I added, "and he worked for you."

"Who's your brother?" the guy asked.

I told him.

"Zwick?" he said. "He was a lying, lazy piece of shit."

The guy waited a few silent seconds for me to say otherwise. I didn't. He hung up.

I saw the truth my son sensed, what he must have been trying to warn me about with his cries. Fort Mac was not for us. The two of us needed serious help and I didn't know who else to turn to. I picked up a bottle of Crown and a case of Canadian and drove to the 7-Eleven I had spotted on the ride into town, situated right across from a strip club. I parked on the block opposite both and, with my son in my arms, turned into the alley behind the Sev.

Laurie, for once, had been right. There were prostitutes. Two of the women sat on chairs they had dragged back there, huddled up in their parkas and sharing a cigarette, while another did her thing, her moaning john shielded by the dumpster. When I said I needed help, the older of the two cackled as she asked if I had a fatal case of blue balls, even though she could see I had a bawling baby in my arms. The younger woman, though, she took my son from my arms and embraced him with real care. It was almost like Laurie, when she made her proclamation about Fort Mac whores and 7-Eleven, had been possessed by some abetting angel, the spirit of my brother, or the more general ghost of wealth and growth.

"He's hungry," the young woman said.

"No," I said, "he won't eat a thing."

"What are feeding him?"

"Juice boxes and canned fruit."

She looked from my boy to me and smiled. "This kid needs milk."

Her name was Lisa. She had a few too many scabs on her face to be considered beautiful, and the way she half-shook, half-fidgeted made me wary about letting her carry my boy, but she did finally bring him peace. She showed me what to buy in 7-Eleven, and, back in the half-ton, she showed me how to prepare a bottle. He took to that nipple straightaway and sucked the whole thing down and slept.

I told Lisa I wanted to reward her with a night on the town, but I didn't think my boy could make it past the bouncers without some top-notch fake ID. Lisa laughed at that and said she would be much happier doing something quieter anyway. I peeled her a few twenties off the wad the journalist had given me. It wasn't that I expected anything from her. I just wanted her to know she wouldn't go home empty-handed and get trouble from whoever she might get trouble from. I drove out to where she told me. The two beers she polished off eased her shake, and, once we found the third spot she suggested unoccupied, we smoked some dope. That calmed her right down. I bundled up my sleeping boy in my parka and laid him in the driver's seat so I could nestle closer to Lisa.

Surrounded by the trees and the dark, she opened up. She opened me right up. I turned the truck on intermittently to warm us and we talked and talked and talked. She told me about the guy she had followed up to Fort Mac. They had been high school sweethearts, but he had died in an accident and his parents took her son. Since then, she had been struggling to quit drugs and alternating between boyfriends who would beat her, boyfriends who would pimp her out and, as was currently the case, boyfriends who did both. I told her about my brother. How he had had a bit of a mental illness and taken his life, and how I thought I might be getting a bit of a mental illness, too, and that if it weren't for my boy I would follow in my brother's footsteps pretty quick. I'd thought Fort Mac would be so much more. Wasn't it booming? I didn't know what the hell to do. Lisa said not to worry about that yet. She kissed me. Her hands rubbed me down there until I burst.

When I drove her to her apartment building, I was so drunk and exhausted I was falling asleep at the wheel. I had just enough left in my tank to ask, "What would you say if I said I'd take you wherever you wanted to go?"

"You don't mean that."

"I do. You're so good with my boy. With me."

She leaned back across the seat and draped her arms around my shoulders.

"I'd love to see the ocean," she said. "I've got a cousin in Vancouver. I'd let you take me there."

"Then stay," I said, hugging her arms, "we'll leave right now."

"There are some things in there I need to take care of," she said, gesturing back to the apartment building, "and some things I don't want to leave behind. But if you wake up this afternoon and still want what you want now, you can pick me up where you found me. My boyfriend usually has me at the 7-Eleven by nine."

I drove back to the hotel and I was about to pull into the parking lot when I spotted the ambulance and the two police cars parked out front, their lights flashing blue and red. I circled the hotel a few times, trying to figure out if they were there for me. Deciding to play it safe, I found a spot a few blocks away to park and sleep. I unwrapped my son from my parka. He fussed for a bit but went right back to sleep. I held him tight in my arms, pulled my jacket over us like a blanket and joined him, eyes closed, in dreaming.

* * *

That was years ago, many jobs ago and spells without jobs, many aliases and fake identities, many moons and seasons. I've apprenticed with a blind locksmith since then, hunted for scrap copper and worked the toxic substance crew at a recycling plant. I manned this beast of a grinder designed to shred the thick plastic barrels that had once carried everything from cancer-giving fire retardants to the blood, urine and fecal samples the hospital had finished testing. I bet that grinder had a bigger number of lethal teeth than all the sharks left on earth combined. The guy who had held the job before me had gone fishing for a stuck metal lid without shutting off the breaker first. They'd had to hose him out. The cops got close to nabbing me a few times, once showing up at a copy centre right after I slipped out to buy smokes, but it has been a while since I've heard anyone come searching for old Zwick. I've sold sports shoes in a shopping mall under the name Hanson. Sid was what I told them to call me when I delivered pizza.

When I left Fort Mac, I never would have guessed I would live to see the end of the week. What happened there gave me a full-blown mental illness and for months all I could think about was joining my brother in eternity. It was a young guy with cancer who saved me. His name was Cam. He couldn't have been more than thirty, but he might as well have been one hundred and thirty for all the time he had left to live. I met him while working as a line cook at a pub out in Fredericton. I had finished for the night and I was sitting down to my usual four pints before heading home and turning my attention to the whisky. Cam looked fresh from the slab of Dr. Frankenstein, one of the failures the good doctor had let free before he got skilled enough to make a proper monster. Cam was in such rough shape I couldn't really say no when he learned I cooked at the pub and asked if I could help him seduce the bartender, Robyn.

He said he had everything he needed in his knapsack, and he unzipped the bag to show me a bundle of wrecked flowers, a bottle of vodka and some CDs with lovers on the front silhouetted by sunsets and candlelight. The promotional key chain he strained to yank off the neck of the vodka was a plastic penguin. He handed it to me and said, "You keep this to remember that guy you helped find love one last time." He wanted a beer so bad, but he had to stay away from glutens because of the medication he took to help him survive his treatment. I wouldn't have been able to play along if Robyn hadn't been such a sweetheart. She assured Cam the stitches tangled dark along the back of his bald skull were not that bad. When he gave her the flowers, she pretended not to see the card stuck in with the petals that read "Get Well."

Cam shared photos with us, mostly of people he hadn't spoken to in years, providing full names for each: first, middle, last. When he saw me fiddling with the penguin key chain, he said, "Those poor, tuxedoed bastards are running out of real estate, that whole global warming deal." Handing Robyn a photo taken near a logging camp, he claimed this really squat guy had tattooed a rooster above one knee, and some almonds above the other, and he would win drinks off people in bars by betting his cock and nuts were all the way down to here. She laughed like she hadn't heard that one a million times.

When I finally couldn't take it anymore, and Robyn grew busier with the midnight rush, I told Cam that, while he was out for a smoke, Robyn had asked me to pass along a message. She wanted him to wait in the stall with the busted toilet. Before I could embellish my lie with any sexy details, he was zipping up his bag and limping off to the bathroom as fast as those faulty legs would carry him. He paused before entering the can to give me a big grin and a thumbs-up. That's when I finally got it. I understood why I couldn't end my life.

It was his look of hope that moved me. There was a similar hope that, as long as I lived, I could help sustain. Just as Cam believed Robyn was about to join him, all those people back home who had known my son believed he was still alive. As long as I didn't turn up dead, the hope would remain that I was out there somewhere raising him, and within that hope he would endure. All those useless folks in Moose Jaw who had known my son – his waste of a mom, her waste of a family, her wasted addict friends, the ladies who ran whatever waste-filled daycare my boy used to get dumped off at, the waste-spreading welfare office he got dragged to so his mommy could get more money on her cheque – could be put to work in their hope. That brought him back to me some, the idea that they still believed my boy was out there, like a new fuel waiting to be discovered, infinitely renewable at best, or, at the very least, not yet burned.

I never returned to the pub. I drifted for a while, thinking about what Cam had shown me. This silence. This need to endure in silence. I have come to terms with my responsibility. I have accepted the fact that I can never let anyone know where my son is buried. I can never tell anyone it wasn't my fault, even though, second by second, this is what I want to do more than anything. It was an accident. I was holding him too close. I must have rolled over on him in my sleep that night, the two of us stuffed into the cramped cab of our truck. He must have wailed and kicked against me. I must have been way too gone to feel or hear a thing.

The only person who ever knew the truth was Lisa. She's dead now, too. I picked her up from behind the 7-Eleven, like we had planned. I tried to put on a fake face, but I couldn't help but let her see I was bawling. I had to show her why. We buried my boy together and we started out for Vancouver, but I could see she was biding her time when she said she loved me and promised to never tell a soul.

I sometimes wonder if I've got things backwards, the way I'm always shitting on shit. What if our culture's contribution to the great big history of everything has been to make the act of creating garbage, to make the act of throwing shit away, the ultimate good? This idea first came to me after I left Cam in the pub. I paused at a garbage can, holding the penguin key chain over the mouth of the bin, wondering if there were any words that could save it. That's when I first got the inkling of this idea. If you hang onto something, you don't make room for what's next. The eleventh commandment our time has chiselled onto the original ten: Thou Shall Make Trash. I chucked the key chain, in case you hadn't guessed. I've junked the idea of getting all depressed when I picture those depleted migrations, those poor flightless fucks sliding across shrinking ice toward a rising sea.

This story will go in the trash, too, just like it always does, as soon as I finish. It's at times like this I can't help but write it, even though I know putting all this down in words is the road to trouble. I'm riding on a Greyhound in between jobs, in between houses and cities and names, and my mind's given room to roam and get the better of me. The writing helps me rope my wild thoughts and fence them in, make a bit of sense of all the senselessness I've survived. It's a kind of ledger, a way to figure out how all in this world that's befallen me measures up against all, in payback, I've befallen on the world. It's a reminder that maybe I'm not the loser everyone has sworn I am since the minute I could listen. Maybe old Zwick the Dick still might come out a winner in the end. I wonder if my boy would be proud of what I've made of us, despite all we've lost. I write about that sometimes, the two of us, imagining our adventures on the road. Imagining he gives me a new nickname, like Zwick the Slick. Or Rad Dad. Even just Dad.

When the bus reaches the next stop, I'll rip these pages out of this notebook, ball them up and, like I've done a hundred times before, toss them in the trash. Maybe I'll stay at that middle-of-nowhere town and look for work. Maybe I'll return to my seat on the bus, maybe start this story again or maybe I'll shut my eyes and decide what to do next.

According to a guy I landscaped with in Windsor, there's an organic farmer in the interior of BC who will feed you for a week and let you camp on his land if you're willing to sabotage crop-dusters. I could see joining in that sabotage, or sabotaging it. Another option is heading back to Alberta. The prop assistant I was sweet on while doing grunt work on a sci-fi movie runs promotions for the University of Calgary's athletics department. In a recent email, she said I had the perfect personality to dress up in the dinosaur costume at sporting events to horse around with the kids and fire up the crowd. It's too late for me to go back to school, but I wouldn't mind taking a class or two to help me get my head around the internet. So much to learn there about what's been and what's coming, and I could find a way to share a bit about what I've experienced and learned, what I see coming. For the longest time, I've wanted to track down the woman my brother wrote about in the first letter he sent me, right after he dropped out of school and escaped up north to plant trees. She was a self-proclaimed "Old Mystic" who would only have anal sex because she wanted her vagina to remain pure and free of men for the child she believed she still might have, despite her age, the anus she claimed bringing him closer to her anyway, putting him into contact with the dark passage through which all she had ever taken in had passed wasted into light.

POEMB

FADE IN:

INT. KITCHEN - NIGHT

JULIA (40) sits at a small kitchen table across from KAVYA (42). Julia holds a notepad and pen and studies Kavya. Kavya is open to Julia's attention, eager for her to speak.

Julia wears a baggy grey T-shirt and shorts for PJs. Her hair is flat and unkempt. Kavya's PJ top and bottoms are brightly coloured. Her full head of curls is well styled. Behind Julia, the kitchen doorway opens on a dark hall. Behind Kavya, a window opens on the night.

Julia continues to study Kavya. Kavya, impatient, finally gives her a look that says, "c'mon" and "so?"

                  JULIA
        (reading from her notepad)
      Kav, you are the night sky: the
      brightness of the stars and the
      fullness of the dark that embraces
      them.

Kavya reacts with surprise mixed with skepticism. Julia tries again.

                  JULIA
      You are the window, providing
      protection and vision.

Kavya, puzzled, glances back at the window behind her. She returns her disappointed gaze to Julia.

                  JULIA
      You are the balm --

                  KAVYA
      An explosive? Seriously, Jules?

                  JULIA
      No, a balm. Like a salve.

                  KAVYA
      Why not both?

POEMB

JULIA
A bomb balm. Or a balm bomb?

KAVYA
A balmb: B-A-L-M-B.

JULIA
That's promising.

Kavya pushes back from the table.

KAVYA
No, Jules, it's dumb. I was just
being dumb.

Julia drops her notepad. Kavya stands and walks
to the window, studying it.

KAVYA
We've known each other how many years
and all you can think to compare me
to is this window?

JULIA
Twenty-two years, Kav. And despite
two decades of evidence to the
contrary you still insist I'm a poet.

Kavya turns back to face Julia.

KAVYA
You are a poet. But right now, it's
like you're writing ad copy on acid.

                    JULIA
My drug days are behind me but I'm
game for an ad: "Is writing poems at
midnight leaving you exhausted? Try
sleep."

                    KAVYA
You'd rather sleep than make my
going-away present?

                    JULIA
I'd rather not make your going-away
present so you can't leave.

                    KAVYA
That means I'll leave without knowing
how wonderful you think I am.

                    JULIA
You know I think you're the most
wondrous. You're brilliant, generous,
beautiful, funny --

Kavya turns back to the window.

                    KAVYA
I asked you to write a poem, not
quote my mother when she complains
she can't understand why I haven't
married.

                    JULIA
Would you feel better if I quoted
what my mom says about me?

Kavya turns back to Julia.

>   KAVYA
>   There's an idea. I can share exactly
>   what makes you wonderful. Help
>   inspire you.

>   JULIA
>   Please don't.

Kavya, her eyes and smile twinkling, sits back
down across from Julia.

>   KAVYA
>   Jules, you are the big breaths we
>   inhale to snorkel under the shadow of
>   that ancient sea turtle.

Julia shakes her head "no."

>   KAVYA
>   You are the heart and will that finds
>   another height to almost beat me at
>   tennis.

>   JULIA
>   Kav.

>   KAVYA
>   Fine. To sometimes beat me at tennis.

>   JULIA
>   I'm being serious, stop.

                    KAVYA
    You are the joy of an eight Negroni
    night and the notes we harmonize at
    karaoke, bringing down the house.

                    JULIA
    I said, stop.

Julia pushes away from the table and withdraws
to the doorway, bracing against the jamb.

                    KAVYA
    It's all true, Jules.

                    JULIA
    Nobody sees that but you.

                    KAVYA
    You just have to show them.

Julia turns back.

                    JULIA
    Now? I'm the broken ankle you
    splinted when we hiked up north,
    except the wound is full-body and
    infected.

                    KAVYA
    Now you stop.

                    JULIA
    I'm the sickness of a sixteen Negroni
    night heaving out of every orifice and
    pore.

POEM B

KAVYA

Don't do this to yourself.

JULIA

I'm not, Kav. You're doing this to me.

These words strike Kavya, pushing her back in
her chair. Hurt, she watches Julia in disbelief.

JULIA

You want a poem? How's this? You're
the window opened on a mile-thick
concrete wall.

Julia moves forward as she speaks, stopping at
her chair but not sitting. Kavya holds her gaze.

JULIA

You're the night that swallows the
sun's last rise.

Kavya's head lowers.

JULIA

You are tonight, Kav. This terrible,
awful night.

Kavya escapes to the window, leaning on it for
support. Julia watches her and then turns and
starts for the hall.

KAVYA

I didn't do this to you.

This stops Julia in the doorway.

> JULIA
> You're abandoning me.

Kavya turns around to face Julia. Julia keeps her back to Kavya.

> KAVYA
> You're the one in the doorway.

> JULIA
> You're the one who pushed me here.

> KAVYA
> All I did was ask for a poem.

Julia turns back to face Kavya.

> JULIA
> So you could make me feel helpless
> and stupid.

Kavya returns to her chair and gestures to the notepad.

> KAVYA
> So we could be together.

Julia steps to her chair, waving away the notepad.

> JULIA
> On a piece of paper?

                    KAVYA
     In a poem.

                    JULIA
     More like a tomb.

Kavya withdraws from this, but then leans
forward again, smiling playfully.

                    KAVYA
     A tomb poem. I like that. Our poemb.

Julia is too surprised to counter.

                    KAVYA
     Like our balm bomb, but with a beret
     and European cigarettes.

Julia loosens, fights off a smile.

                    KAVYA
     P-O-E-M-B. Poem-b!

Julia, laughing, sits.

                    JULIA
     You're so dumb. I love you.

Kavya places her hands on the notepad.

                    KAVYA
     And we will be safe on this page
     together in our dumbness and love.

Julia takes Kavya's hands. Kavya flashes a wry
smile.

> JULIA
> Don't say it again.

> KAVYA
> In our poemb.

They both laugh.

> JULIA
> So, more dumbness than love.

They laugh again.

MOM (68) calls down from upstairs, drawing their
attention. Their hands separate.

> MOM (O.S.)
> Are you still up, honey?

Julia turns from the doorway back to Kavya. Kavya
gives her that twinkling smile.

> JULIA
> I'm working on my poem for Kavya, Mom.

> MOM (O.S.)
> You should get a good night's sleep
> before tomorrow.

Julia continues to meet Kavya's gaze. Kavya
smiles and nods in a way that says, "You got
this." Julia fights to keep it together.

POEMB

The seat Kavya occupied is empty, the window
fully visible in her absence.

As Julia remains seated alone at the kitchen
table, the sound from tomorrow's funeral rises
-- the end of a song. Julia continues to watch
the empty spot Kavya had occupied.

> CELEBRANT (V.O.)
> Kavya's best friend, Julia, will now
> share a poem she wrote to celebrate
> Kavya's life.

Julia, still seated at the kitchen table, grabs
the notepad and writes.

> JULIA (V.O.)
> This is for you, my dear Kav. For
> what I will miss the most: the way
> you never told any of us what we
> should be, but always believed deeply
> in what we could do.

As Julia writes, Kavya's chair at the kitchen
table remains empty, the window clear with
night.

> JULIA (V.O.)
> It's called "Poemb."

FADE OUT.

DEAR ADOLF

He calls out dig this earth deeper you lot there
you others sing now and play.
– Paul Celan

INTRODUCTION

ALMA FORGE WAS THE LAST REMAINING SIGN OF THE
park. She began running her tours back in July of 2010. She led
visitors through the south Saskatchewan fields where the park
once stood, telling the story of the birth of Shoahville and giving
her take on its untimely demise.

I was doing research for a series of poems I planned to write
from the perspective of Alma's father when I discovered an article
about her tours. I reached out to her and we spoke by phone twice
in March of 2011. She sounded skeptical about my interest in her

father but was forthcoming nonetheless, sharing her version of the park's rise and fall and discussing what she saw as her father's motivation for backing the Shoahville project. At the end of our second conversation, she told me if I really wanted to experience the truth, I needed to take her tour. I agreed. I booked a spot with her for late April when I planned to fly to Saskatchewan anyway to visit my folks.

Engrossed in the bounty of material Alma had given me, I began work on my poems about her father and didn't end up calling her again until I arrived in the Prairies. I tried her a few days after getting settled on my parents' farm, first at home and then, after a recorded voice told me the number was disconnected, at the diner where she waited tables. The manager told me he'd fired her after she bailed on another shift, most likely because of what he called "her crazy commitment to that stupid park." He had not heard from her since.

The time I had intended to spend with family went to Alma instead. I talked to everyone who knew her, which ended up being mostly former co-workers from the diner, the university or the park. They all had a rumour. Alma was holed up in a cabin she owned in northern Manitoba and she was finally writing that book in defence of her dad. She was living in Nova Scotia with long-forgotten relatives from her mother's side, cleansing herself of her father's crimes. She had taken off to Hollywood and was having her tour adapted into a feature-length film. The guy who washed dishes at the diner said powerful government forces wanted the park to go away forever and had snuffed her out. I ran this story by Harriet Vervalcke, Alma's former partner, who herself had settled on the west coast, and she informed me the dishwasher also believed there were catacombs west of town flush with lost Cree gold and that the Yanks were using guillotines to off criminals because beheadings allowed them to effectively harvest organs for our extraterrestrial masters.

As the rumours about Alma's whereabouts became more discordant, offering less promising leads, I realized a significant pattern had emerged. The plethora of rumours was matched by the abundance of references to Alma's dedication to maintaining the local memory of her father and the park. And with each story about her missing a shift at the diner to take a single curious visitor on the tour, with each mention of her pouring the few pennies she had into this venture, I became more and more absorbed. I began to ask what Alma must have asked: after creating a global sensation, and after destroying her father, how could Shoahville be erased from its prairie home? What struck me with as much force as the mystery of Alma's disappearance was the thought of what had been lost with her loss. I had no choice but to pursue it.

I started my work on Wednesday, May 11. I interviewed Harriet and the locals who had been involved in the park, or the ones who would admit to it, at least. I also tracked down and interviewed – in person, by phone, via email and Skype – locals and tourists who had taken Alma's tour. I probed them for details about what Alma had said and done, where she had led them. I searched for a sense of how she had sought to shape their experience and why. I asked them to share every photo and video they had shot while taking the tour. When I had as clear of a picture of the tour as could be expected, I took the tour myself. On Saturday, June 4, I set out on an overcast morning and visited the sites I would have visited had Alma still been present to be my guide.

The work that follows is my attempt to preserve Alma's attempts at preservation. Drawing on my research, I have composed a speculative transcript of the words Alma might have spoken while performing her tours. With my rendering of her voice, you can visit the site and take your own makeshift tour. You can visit the land where Alma no longer leads her charges through the immensity of what no longer stands.

Daniel Scott Tysdal
Toronto, ON
(August 2011)

TOUR STOP #1: THE LAND

Learn this: my dad was not an evil man.

Put yourselves behind his eyes for a minute. This is where he stood that damp, windy morning in April of 2006. Wednesday the nineteenth to be exact. Imagine the land is as flat and far-reaching then as it is right now. Imagine it's just as vacant. The Mikalski Brothers are on either side of you. Look to your left: there's Zygmunt. Urban's on your right. Straight up ahead, their camera crew films your every step.

Now imagine you can't help but feel sorry for these Polish boys as you navigate the undeveloped soil your family has farmed since settling in Saskatchewan in the spring of 1891, the land still known then as the North-West Territories. Partly you pity them because they truly are a pair of fish out of water. Zygmunt stops every few paces to scrape the mud from his crocodile leather loafers with a rolled-up newspaper, while the metallic sheen of Urban's suit doesn't look native to this planet, let alone the Prairies. Mostly, though, you feel sorry for them because they are too young – late twenties biologically, but mid-teens in terms of their business acumen – to know how to deliver a winning pitch. The brothers have got a one-of-a-kind vision for your land, but they spend more time mugging for their camera crew than they do bringing this vision to life. Urban falls back on empty abstractions like "revolutionary," "indispensable," "groundbreaking," his Slavic accent manoeuvring the syllables into new regions of cadence and intonation.

Zygmunt stops scraping at the mud on his shoes long enough to smile up at you and ask, "Mr. Forge, is this not the perfect home for Shoahville?"

Before you answer, "No," folks, imagine, like my dad, their story is coursing through you like it's your own blood. It's the story of two Polish Jews who want to create the first truly twenty-first-century Holocaust memorial. They were spurred to action by the recent death of their great-grandfather, a survivor of the Belzec extermination camp. Imagine you are painfully aware – though not at all surprised – their monumental vision has not been grasped by the other cities they solicited for support: Calgary, Edmonton, Winnipeg and Saskatoon. Imagine knowing in your bones you are their last hope. Having built a specialty crop empire, and having made a killing during the Alberta oil boom, you're the only one with the land, the financial clout and the government connections to get it done. More importantly, you are a student of history, of this century, what it wrought and what it ruined, and you know well and good the suffering you have been spared. Imagine that what eats at you more and more with each passing year, with the withering of the number of seasons left to you as you near seventy, is how little you have done to give thanks for all your blessings, to give back to those who were not spared. And now imagine the camera crew that's been documenting every second of Urban and Zygmunt's fruitless mission has you in its grip. The lens seizes you.

Zygmunt stops fooling with the mud on his shoes and asks, "Is this not the perfect home?"

Let your head fill with the thought my dad's head filled with. This memorial is your chance to finally give back, your chance to finally leave a lasting mark for the Forge family name, for the Prairies, even for every soul that lives and breathes in this very era and needs the future to remember that, yes, we remembered. Because Shoahville *is* the natural, necessary evolution. That's how the Mikalskis put it. What was once oral transforms into print. What was once made for the stage speeds to the small and the big screens. The atrocities of the past need a new form of witness or Nazi hate will be free to repeat. The museum is not enough.

Zygmunt asks, "Is this not perfect?"

Say it with me, folks.

What my dad said.

Say, "Yes."

Say, "Wow."

Pop quiz: Was he evil?

TOUR STOP #2: THE ENTRANCE

Here's some food for thought before we step onto the spot where Shoahville once stood. When my dad visited me after sealing the deal with the Mikalskis and said, "Alma, I'm backing a Holocaust-themed amusement park," I called him disgusting, dim-witted and mad as a mule is stubborn. His only daughter. I called him evil. Who would have thought that by opening day I would know the park like it was my own flesh and blood?

Learn this, folks: it was my partner, Harriet, who proposed the two of us take jobs at Shoahville. She pitched the plan in June of 2008 right where you're standing. Harriet, at forty-seven, was five years my senior. According to her, that meant she had final say over what we imagined we would do with our millions when we finally won the 6/49 and which toppings to order on the second pizza at 2-4-1. In June of '08, this very spot was the entrance to what the promotional material dubbed "the greatest innovation in Holocaust remembrance" but what the two of us smartasses called "atroci-tainment" and "enter-travesty." The park, at that time, was still not completed, a bad winter having delayed construction and pushed the grand opening back to the fall.

Here's how Harriet's proposal came about. On Wednesday, June 4, 2008, a year and a bit after Dad and I had last spoken, Dad called me. That had been our longest extended silence, and the first silence Dad had ever broken. Harriet was to thank for that because she had refused to let me cave. In the past, I had always felt guilty after Dad and I had a blow-up. I could be counted on to call him within a week to make amends. After I had lost it on him over Shoahville, though, Harriet had said she would walk straight out the door and not look back if I called him.

"What he is doing is unforgivable, Alma," she would say each time I nearly gave in, "and he never listens to you anyway. So why bother calling?"

She was right, of course. Dad had never listened to me. When I was twelve, he refused to come home early from a business trip in the States. I told him Mom was going to pass soon, but the doctors had assured him before he left that she had months to live. There was even a chance she would regain consciousness and beat the cancer. She breathed her last breath the next night. When I was eighteen, I begged Dad to talk to Marv, my older brother and only sibling, about his hard partying. Dad scowled at me like I was the one blowing paycheques on rounds for the boys, all-night card games and Hells Angels cocaine. Oats needed to be sowed, Dad explained. Marv was killed, and the woman he had been cheating on his fiancée with was left a vegetable, when a train obliterated Marv's car. The two of them had been too drunk to realize Marv had parked on the tracks when they drove out past the city limits to screw around. When I finished high school, Dad forced me to enrol in Business at the University of Saskatchewan, even though all I had ever talked about studying was art, and the "compromise" we reached, History, had been his second choice. And when I moved back home from the west coast after finishing grad school and finally came out to my dad, he still kept setting me up with divorced hired hands and the most hopeless sons of his business partners. He would plead innocence, confessing he'd thought I had said something about having grown out of "that phase." Shoahville was no different. It was bad news, I told him. Who couldn't see that? He couldn't, evidently, and the more I witnessed his blindness to the horror of the park, the more deeply I believed I would never speak to him again.

When my cell rang that Wednesday in June of 2008, the last voice I expected to hear on the other end was Dad's saying, "Hey there, Alma girl." My astonishment at the call was quickly replaced by disappointment, though, when Dad apologized profusely for his extended silence. The apology itself was an aberration. If a cartoon caveman version of Dad had invented the square wheel, he would have stuck with his immobile vehicle rather than admit he was wrong when round wheels were discovered. The fact that his apology came without caveats or goading told me he was only calling because he needed my help. I was alone in the office I shared at the university with other temporary faculty, but I could still feel my eyes rolling and my face smirking, as if to signal to my invisible audience, "Can you believe this man?" It was a struggle to resist the urge to hang up. I pushed aside a pile of unmarked Introduction to History papers, leaned on my desk, and added, as needed, monosyllabic affirmative and negative replies.

Dad finally finished his apology and pitched his problem: he was in Toronto and he needed me to pick up Grandpa from Shoahville. Grandpa's truck wouldn't start and no one at the park had the guts to drive him home. Grandpa had been caught by security taking a sledgehammer to the Schutzstaffel Tilt-a-Whirl, his second attack in as many weeks. The Friday previous, he had stormed into the Winston Churchill Allied History Museum to retrieve his old WWII service rifle, which Dad had put on display without his permission, sending the actor who played Stalin to the hospital with a palpitating heart and rousing a dispatch from the RCMP that ended with the phrase "possible hostage situation."

I agreed to pick up Grandpa for Grandpa's sake, but Dad took my affirmative as a peace offering and bubbled with excitement about his trip to Toronto. The night before, he had received the 2008 Wiesel Holocaust Education and Awareness Award from the Canadian chapter of the B'nai Brith. One of the distinguished presenters, he boasted, had praised his insightful courage in the face of blind global resistance, his shining originality in this dark, insipid age. To top it all off, at the end of the ceremony Urban and Zygmunt had made a surprise announcement: they were donating to the park the diary their great-grandfather had kept hidden during his internment in Belzec. I congratulated Dad and asked if the news of the diary had warmed the hearts of any of the protesters who had gathered outside the convention hall to greet him. "Or did you and the Mikalskis ask the police to intervene?"

"That's not fair," Dad said and went quiet.

Back in '06, in response to the opposition to the park, the Mikalski brothers had lobbied local officials to pass a bylaw banning protests within a twenty-five-kilometre radius of a construction site – for safety reasons, of course. Every few weeks there would be arrests, most often involving members of the multi-faith assembly that opposed the park's cultural genocide or the First Nations coalition that demanded a simple museum dedicated to remembering the genocide committed against their people on this very land.

"You'd better go get Grandpa," Dad said after a long pause, and then added, "Call me to let me know how he's doing."

He gave me his number. "You can let me know how you're keeping, too."

"I will," I said, and hung up.

Harriet picked me up at the university. She had been at work at the CBC, editing a piece on garage sale tips for the evening news. She was happy to pass the work off to a colleague so she could tend to a family emergency, especially an emergency that would give us our first close look at Shoahville. What you need to realize, folks, is that as we drove to the park to pick up Grandpa – passing the city limits, the sign-pocked ditches, the booth of the parking lot – the journey was accomplished increment-by-increment, mile-by-mile. However, as we approached, Shoahville itself underwent an exponential intensification. Right here where you're standing, Harriet's jaw outright dropped and it stayed slapped open, as though the Loch Ness monster had surfaced out of the earth strapped to Cthulhu's head.

We had seen the park at a distance, peering out the back window of Grandpa's place about six miles that way. I had seen the construction from a plane once. That was the previous March, in '07, when Dad flew me to see him in New York while he canvassed investors on behalf of the Mikalski brothers and defended them and the park in the press. The position of vice-president was mine, he said, and not just because I was family. He needed a reliable, gifted and imaginative second-in-command. He had a soft spot for the Mikalskis, particularly Zygmunt, who was fastidious like Mom, but the brothers were about as useful as two holes in the head when it came to conducting business.

"Acting like fools for the cameras," as Dad put it, "is the one thing you can count on those boys to accomplish."

Despite Dad's criticism, he, like the Mikalskis, was happy to be followed everywhere by a camera crew. I had to threaten to leave without hearing his pitch to get him to ask the crew to take a break. Like Urban, Dad had also taken to speaking in grandiose abstractions about the park's "revolutionary" and "groundbreaking" potential. All he was missing was the Polish accent. He had me close my eyes and picture a globally minded world in which our community, our family and our roots defined the future of the preservation of the past. Shoahville was just the start. I'd made the trip to let him know I thought he was killing Grandpa. I told him so. The ensuing screaming match marked the beginning of what would become our more than year-long silence. On the flight back, the half-finished amusement park hadn't looked like much more than a ball of lint dotting the patchwork blanket of sown and unsown fields. Or a tuft of brambles on a path a thousand miles wide.

Up close, though? When it was done? Visualize it with me. Where you see nothing but dirt and sky, folks, see this: a bramble, sure, but one that's been growing since the beginning of time and somewhere along the line it mixed its lineage, cross-pollinating with a colony of industrial machines. Or picture how a tangle of barbed wire would loom if you were shrunk to three inches tall. Straight ahead of you, see the iron of the entrance twisted with the welcome "*Schauspiel macht frei*" – "play liberates" – though, folks, note they had meant to pick the verb "to play," not the noun "play." And just beyond that flub see the oh-so-sanctimonious Mikalski Brothers' Visitor Centre. To the left, the screaming peak of the Tod Train Supercoaster snaps at your eyes, while right up there the periscope that tops the U-Boat Indoor Water Park tracks your every move. And rising out of the centre of this aberrant mass is all two hundred feet of Remembrance Tower, the quasi-obelisk crowned with the rainbow glow of the Shoahville logo.

I've got buttons with the logo back in the van, if you'd like. I made them myself, as a keepsake to help you remember the tour. Remind me, and you can each have one at no extra charge. Dad had meant for the logo to be a sun, but it ended up looking more like a flower, so he went with that. The yellow Jewish star makes the centre of the bloom, and the petals are formed by the different-coloured triangles the Nazis used to mark the rest of the victims in the camps. Picture that atrocity. Picture it rising way, way up at my dad's command. At night, it was visible for miles.

Say, "Wow," folks.

Say, "My God."

Pop quiz: Was he evil?

That was the question Harriet asked on this very spot in June of 2008 and immediately answered, "Yes." She led me away from the booth at the entrance of Shoahville so she could make her pitch in private, the guard behind us drawling into his walkie-talkie, "They're here to pick up gramps." Harriet's spiel came with such ease I knew right away she'd been scheming for months, even though we had both promised to abandon the pipe dream of stopping Shoahville. In those first months, back when the park was a concept, there had been so many voices of protest that ours had not been needed. But then as fast as you can say, "lemming," Dad had gathered such a hammering mass of local then provincial then national support we knew if our rebellious voices reached a certain volume they would be quashed. More and more often Harriet was forced to edit together segments praising Shoahville – The jobs! The tourists! The historical import! – for the CBC News, and more and more I was asked by students hunting for work in everything from performance to construction if I would put in a good word for them with Dad.

It was while editing a puff piece on the Mikalski brothers' documentary crew that Harriet had had her epiphany. The park was powered by opinion. That was how she put it. So we needed to redirect the power of that opinion against the park. We needed to document every wrong we could. We needed to catch that one reprehensible and revolting act that would change the hearts of all those who believed in Shoahville and all those whose indifference caused as much bad as the belief. We needed to land jobs at Shoahville and secretly make the film that would reduce the park to ruins. Great film had changed. What audiences needed now was a *cause*, not a bazillion-dollar budget, period costumes, state-of-the-art CGI and an Oscar-winning cast that retreated to a mansion in the Alps to rehearse for three months. You needed an eye for injustice more than an eye for well-framed and perfectly lit glitz.

Harriet had raged against mainstream movies for as long as I had known her, and she had poked away at a few environmentalist documentary proposals of her own, but I had never seen her speak so passionately about taking up her camera again and fighting back. I had been certain her one experience heading up a commercial film had done her in. It happened a few years before we met, when a decade of shooting ads for local car dealerships and bowling alleys finally paid off. She received a hundred-thousand-dollar budget from the Saskatchewan Communications Network and an independent production company to make a film about a teenage lesbian coming of age in a rural town. The producer pulled the plug before Harriet had finished shooting. Harriet wrote a letter to the *Leader-Post* accusing SCN of being homophobic and misogynistic. The producer replied with a letter written in her own defence. Filming shut down, she explained, because the early footage looked amateurish and two cast members had quit, claiming the director was abusive and combative. Soon after the publication of this letter, Harriet had taken the job editing the local news.

"I want this bad," Harriet said, taking my hands at the entrance to Shoahville. "I want us to get these jobs, make our film and bring this awful place down."

"Me, too," I said, "but Dad will know I'm lying."

"Not if he wants to believe you're telling the truth."

Security finally escorted Grandpa to the entrance. His grimace gave way to a mischievous grin when he spotted us. He greeted us with kisses on the cheek.

"Why the Tilt-a-Whirl?" I asked, taking his arm.

"Yeah, Grandpa," Harriet added, taking his other arm, "why not that godawful tower?"

"I was looking to take a round out of my boy's office, but I got lost."

We drove into town to check on Grandpa's truck, which had been towed to Walker's, and to pick up our usual: Chinese takeout from the Uptown and a six-pack of Boh. On the ride out to Grandpa's place, we told him he could stop trying to dismantle the park one bolt at a time. Protesting didn't work like that. You couldn't force people to change. You needed to show them why and how, to move them to change. We shared our plan. His face screwed up once: when Harriet referred to our film as a "node for activists" and he asked, "What's an ode to Mexicans?" Other than that, he listened intently as Harriet spoke about how our documentary film was going to inspire this change. His arm rested on the open window, sending smoke and ash into the dust the truck kicked up on a road I bet he'd travelled tens of thousands of times in his eighty-eight years, firing how many measures of smoke and spit and snot and whistled tunes and silence into the ditches and the prairie air.

"You think you're going to stop that thing with pictures?" he asked.

"That's one way to put it." I laughed.

"You're starting to sound as crazy as your dad," he cracked in return.

Still ablaze with Harriet's passionate plea, I stayed in the car to call Dad. Harriet and Grandpa carried the beer and Chinese up to the house, a two-storey brick beauty built by my greatgrandpa in 1925 with bricks, I'm proud to digress, fired in the brickworks factory my great-great-grandfather opened with a group of investors south of here in 1910. Eighty-plus years later, the house was on its last legs. Grandpa had been too slowed by age for the last decade to re-shingle the roof or patch the foundation and too proud for the last five years to let Dad pay for its repair. Grandpa knelt in the tall grass that encircled the house and held out an egg roll, trying to coax his old mutt, Link (short for Lincoln), out from a hole in the porch. I pieced together my fake pitch from all the bull Dad would want to hear about family, the Prairies and the future. So weak in the hips, Link could barely stand and had to inch across the ground to reach his treat.

Once Harriet, Grandpa and Link were inside, I dialled. The phone rang and my excitement was tempered by fear. My lungs tightened. My underarms poured sweat. I was afraid Dad would grasp the real motivation behind my sudden change of heart as easily as a burrowed hare's claws find dirt. Dad answered and asked about Grandpa. I was afraid I would let Harriet down. My mind rattled with answers to the probing questions I was certain Dad was going to hit me with. I was afraid this was our one chance and we had left it too late. We had waited too long to say, "No."

I managed a weak "Grandpa is Grandpa."

"What about you? Are you okay?" Dad asked.

He knows I'm a fake, was what I thought. He knows, he knows, he knows.

"Alma?"

"Harriet and I were wondering something," I said.

"What's that?"

"We were wondering if you were still hiring."

Before I could launch into all the made-up reasons we had for wanting what we wanted for real, Dad cut me off.

"This B'nai Brith award I've been carrying on about," he said, "is a speck of ant shit beside the prize of you asking to sign up to fight the good fight. You just tell me what I can do."

The next morning, Harriet gave her notice at the CBC. I abandoned my students mid-semester and withdrew my applications to teach at the university in the fall. A few days later, on the tenth of June 2008, Harriet and I were back here at the entrance of the park, officially employed.

Harriet was one of Shoahville's eleven field documentarians. When the park finally opened in September, she would be rented out by families, couples and classes of all ages on daylong trips who wanted to document their games of Whack-a-Gestapo and their flights on the 3-D thrill ride, Race to Liberation. When the visitors' journeys were finished, Harriet would edit the footage, creating an overpriced souvenir the advertisements pitched as "the only way to truly never forget."

For my part, I told Dad I was ready to take my spot as his right-hand woman. With Harriet at ground level, I needed to be behind the scenes to give our plan the best chance to succeed. Dad didn't co-operate. I was hired as one of the hundred or so Shoahville tour guides. Dad spun the position as giving me a "greater grasp of the nuts and bolts" before moving me up top, though I think I was being punished for saying no the first time. As I'm sure you folks can glean from my performance today, the goal of the tours was immersion. The guy who trained us had run the Liberty Trolleys, which visited the American Revolution battlefields of Lexington and Concord, and he had worked at Gettysburg, where in the span of two hours he plunged folks like you into the hearts and minds of the men who clashed in the most important battle of the American Civil War.

Joe Earl was his name. He was one of those people who freeze in a certain moment in time. He had fought in Vietnam and he still had this old Elvis look to him, like he was on vacation from a magazine forty years out of date, or like he was nervous about changing to suit the present because he was convinced time would run in reverse as abruptly and unstoppably as it had rushed ahead. I went for beers with him a couple of times. He had flown bomber planes during the war. Lots of times when they finished a mission, he said, there were bombs left over, and they would dump those extra bombs into the jungle, from way up there, wherever they saw fit.

TOUR STOP #3: REDEMPTION SQUARE

Imagine entering the park on that first day of work and searching. Follow me past the spot where the entrance once stood and imagine that, instead of summerfallow and calf-high durum, shops and rides and games and exhibits engulf you. It's your second day and you're searching. Your third: you search. The whole first week, the whole first month, the whole summer you search and search and search for signs. You search for the facts that prove Shoahville is flat-out wrong. Keep moving. What do you see? Now if you're me, the whole thing is a sign. Every last "attraction," whether it's the Private Life of the Master Race Revue or the Beast of Buchenwald House of Horrors or the Maharal Carousel with its chariots, leopards, eagles, gazelles, lions and golems all hollowed out with seats for one or two riders.

Now if you're Harriet – and we can stop here, folks, on the patch of land that once buoyed the park's centre, Redemption Square – your problem isn't with Shoahville, exactly. Sure, you're steamed at not receiving permission to interview Dad, which ends up being the exclusive province of the Mikalski brothers' camera crew. What cripples you if you're Harriet is looking back, trying to select shots from the archival footage of Nazi Germany, Nazi-occupied countries and the Nazi-built camps to juxtapose with the material you catch at the park.

Visualize this: you need to select a seven-second clip from old footage of Romani children. Seven seconds. That's it. You watch the Romani children having their faces measured to determine their racial purity, Romani children mugging for the camera at lunch, Romani children at play in the courtyard of the Catholic-run home where they were held until the study was done and they were transported to Auschwitz. It feels strange – stupid, even – doesn't it? Selecting seven seconds from a stream that refuses to be cut. Nothing will let go. It's necessary, all of it: every ruler raised to measure every patiently stilled forehead and nose; every inch measured between eyes, between the eyes and the mouth; every

swipe of the brush on every boot from the pile of leather the children polish, the brushes doubling as toy daggers for the boys who
playfully fake war; the invigorated gaze of that girl at the lunch
table unfolding playfully, too, as she glances from the camera to a
friend to the camera and back to the friend as if to say, "Look, look,
look. We're being saved."

Learn this, folks: by Friday, September 12, 2008, the day
before the park's grand opening, our film did not have a single
frame. Not one. We'd quit talking about the project altogether
by August. I didn't dare invite Harriet to discuss her field documentarian responsibilities. The last time I'd asked she said she had
been assigned the crucial task of adding sound to an animated
promotional short. "Tell me," she had asked back, "how does a cat
dressed as an SS officer yowl after catching its whiskers in a train
door?" On the morning of September the twelfth, Harriet walked
me to my rehearsal on her way to the studio. She mentioned she
had visited the CTV News HR page. They were looking for an
experienced editor in Victoria. The deadline for applications was
the end of the month. The ocean sounded about right.

This is where she left me to rehearse that morning, folks,
Redemption Square. What you can't see is the Canon Makeshift
Memorial Wall, fifteen feet that way, waiting for visitor-created
cards, poems, pictures, stuffed animals and bouquets. Five feet from
us in the other direction sits the Osmond Earl Forge Memorial
Hall, which was more of a room than a hall, where Dad exhibited
a few family mementos, a number of awards he had received for
founding the park and the Holocaust diary the Mikalski brothers had donated. Twenty-five feet straight behind you balances
the steel base of Remembrance Tower. Now, a little before eleven,
after two hours spent watching the dancers and mobile orchestra
practise their routine, "Saved Welcome Saviour," I stood on this
very spot, ready to finally step into a float shaped like an oversized
oven. The next morning, at the grand opening, this tractor-trailer-
sized monstrosity, covered in yellow crocuses and western red lilies
and filled with Shoahville's guides, would pull up the rear of the

visitor-welcoming parade. When the dance routine finished and the marching band fell silent, we guides would emerge from the float and lead these first visitors on the first tours of the park.

Dad was at the rehearsal, which was a first. He looked nervous in a way I'd never seen, his face and torso all bunched up like he was a piece of paper scribbled with a bad idea. The dancers dispersed and the director shouted for us to assemble in the float. We formed a line and entered in pairs. It was slow going with the oversized striped pyjamas tripping some up. The costumes had been designed to make us appear emaciated, but we ended up looking like children playing the worst game of make-believe imaginable. I was stepping into the packed enclosure, and moaning about how goddamned hot it was, when it happened. The blast. It resounded like nothing else. It was like two tornadoes had funnelled up out of the earth to suck my eardrums down to the soil. Fire like the tail of some bright, fleeting bird brushed the side of the float and just like that the float went up in flames.

Memory in these moments can lose its legs and grasp at a single sensation like it's the stable seat in a runaway train. I don't remember escaping the float. Or calling the fire department. Or forcing my way back into the float to rescue the guy who'd been felled by the smoke. All I recall is hearing Dad. Hearing my dad's voice crying out in a pattern too mangled to turn into words. The mass I pushed through fought the flames, or fought to escape them, or fought to keep me from reaching right over there, where my dad struggled to drag someone away from the source of the blaze, the Osmond Earl Forge Memorial Hall. That sound poured out of Dad. The burned arm of the body he rescued appeared more fungal than flesh. I recognized that face. I finally understood what Dad howled: "Daddy, Daddy, Daddy, no." I performed CPR and got Grandpa breathing. Help arrived. The flames were contained.

I rode to the hospital in the front seat of Grandpa's ambulance. Dad promised to meet me there. Urban and Zygmunt were at the chamber of commerce, preparing for a pre-opening gala cocktail hour with local hotshots and visiting dignitaries. The brothers would panic when Dad didn't show. He had to let them know what happened. But what had happened? I called Harriet from the waiting room. Why might I have done that, folks? To let her know I was safe? Yes. To tell her Grandpa was hurt so bad your heart broke looking at him? Yes. To beg her to hurry to the hospital and hold me tight? For sure, for sure, for sure. But I also needed her to track down one fact for me. You see, a perk of Harriet's position was access to select security cameras to help provide material for her movie mementos. She found the footage I was after.

"Oh, God," she said, and she confirmed the worst. Grandpa had done it. He'd blown up the Osmond Earl Forge Memorial Hall. Harriet confirmed what we didn't know needed confirming. Something worse than the worst. She made a copy of the footage and emailed the clip to a former colleague at the CBC.

"They're running with it at six," she said, calling me back. "We did it. The park is done."

TOUR STOP #4: THE NEWS

Walk with me to the threshold. Right about here, folks. What once stood open on this very spot was the door to the Osmond Earl Forge Memorial Hall. Let's go back to that morning of the rehearsal, remaining in this entrance, and try to see what no security camera could capture. A camera had been installed in the hall, but it had not yet been hooked up due to the hall's last-minute addition to the park.

We know from the footage recorded by the security camera on the shop perpendicular to the hall, the footage Harriet watched and sent to the CBC, that Grandpa slipped in undetected and left the door open. But what he did inside? Imagine him take in the wall of family photos or imagine him ignore them. Imagine him hesitate, think it over, say, "No, no, no, not this, not now," or imagine him straightaway go at exploding. Imagine the thing misfiring.

That's what the fire department confirmed after examining the device. Get in close and reach in and touch where the casing of his homemade incendiary was weak along the top. Feel the blast burst out in a stream, a cut jugular's eruption, more like a flame-thrower than the grenade-like charge Grandpa had designed to wipe out that venue and himself.

Now, imagine my father rushing in. Imagine my father sees his father. See him seeing the smoke and flames mounting so bad he has to act fast. My dad scurries past his dad and lifts the clear container, the size of a cake box, say, that holds the death camp diary of the great-grandfather of Zygmunt and Urban Mikalski. Here's what you would see if you watched the footage recorded by the security camera outside the hall: my father enters the blaze and rescues a box. The second time he enters he comes out with the body of the man who is his dad.

Say it with me, folks.

Say, "Wow."

Say, "You vile piece of shit."

Harriet and I staked out a television in the waiting room at the hospital. It was a little after four and Dad had still not shown up or called. The smoke, according to the doctor, had done more damage than the fire. Grandpa's condition had stabilized post-surgery, but he might have gone too long without air to fully recover. I stood behind Harriet with my arms wrapped around her waist. She was a bit taller than me so my head could rest at a comfortable angle on her shoulder. With the local CBC News still two hours from exposing Dad, she had switched the waiting room television to a twenty-four-hour news station to get an update on the fire. The story of the moment was the bankruptcy of a billion-dollar financial institution, though one of the strata of scrolling text on the screen did read, "Shoahville fire contained, injures six."

"We can just go, Harriet," I said without lifting my face off her warmth.

"You need to be with Grandpa," she said.

"I mean after he's out of the hospital. This isn't home anymore. Not his. Not ours."

"But it will be. People are going to see this footage. They're going to see your dad abandon to the flames, to fucking fire, his own father. This changes everything, Alma. People are going to see."

Know this, folks: we believed Shoahville was done. What we quickly learned was we had missed the whole thing, the exposure, the revelation. It happened that fast, the fall of the risen and their return to rising. The clip Harriet emailed to the local CBC had been forwarded to the national newsroom, and then snuck to a competitor, and then leaked on the internet. And then it went viral.

The Mikalski brothers, for the first time since the park broke ground, faced adversity without Dad's help. And they rose to the challenge by doing the last thing you would expect someone in their shoes to do: they encouraged the footage's spread. Everyone in the park's PR department, every member of their personal documentary crew, conducted that spread online. And every single version of the security camera footage linked to the video of Dad's apology, which had been recorded at the chamber of commerce cocktail party to appear to be a random act, as though an inspired invitee had raised his personal camera out of the crowd to film. Surrounded by the city's business leaders, local politicians and bigwigs from out of town, but no reporters, of course, since this was a private function, Dad confessed. The security footage of what he called the biggest mistake of his life was projected onto the big screen behind him. Gasps were audible. The screen went dark.

Normally, Dad spoke off the cuff, but that day he read from a statement the Mikalski brothers had prepared for him. He could barely make it through two phrases without breaking up. It was unforgivable, he admitted, so he did not want to be forgiven. What he wanted was for us to remember the park. Why we had come together as a community to bring it to life. Remember the message of hope we wanted to preserve for future generations. He told the story about the time he was eight years old and he snuck out in the night to hunt the wolf man with his father's old service rifle. He ended up downing a ten-month-old Simmental bull instead. Rather than laying a licking on him, or giving him his brother's chores for a month, his dad had taken him and the Lee-Enfield rifle to the nuisance ground where they shot at bottles and gophers, his father telling him, "If you're going to hunt, you should at least be able to shoot straight." "The lesson, I guess," Dad finished, "is that you can dislike a man for his bad actions, but don't hate him for his heartfelt aim." He asked the crowd to continue supporting the park and to keep his father in their prayers.

Maybe Dad didn't want it, but he won it. Forgiveness. He brought down the house.

All of this had happened while Harriet and I were at the hospital waiting for the news to break. It was around five when we finally learned we had missed it. While we watched the experts on the twenty-four-hour news station forecast a vicious financial storm, we read this line of scrolling text: "Forge, Shoahville, respond to shocking video."

Immediately, Harriet called her friend at the CBC newsroom. At her friend's recommendation, we tracked the video's spread, site by site. When the six o'clock news finally began, the hosts did not kick off with the damning security tape. They led with the story about the story, the story of this phenomenon: the phenomenon of the crime coupled with the apology; how quickly, united, they proliferated. "The real lesson," one expert put it, "is how the double punch of the wrong and its righting can inspire such a deep outpouring of forgiveness." The park was unaffected. It would open, on schedule, the next day. Dad, the Mikalskis and Shoahville had survived.

It's odd the things you regret when you're helpless. At eight o'clock, the nurse let us into the ICU to visit Grandpa. He was still unconscious. I was overwhelmed by this terrible sense of failing him. This feeling sickened the stomach of every cell in me from head to toe. It wasn't that we had blown our chance with the security tape. It had to do with this documentary for a Remembrance

Day contest Harriet and I had started making back in 2001, when we first moved in together. Even though Grandpa never wanted to say boo about the war, he had opened up for us. As long as one of us helped him paint outbuildings and fix fences while he talked, he had been happy to share stories about being nineteen and getting so little training and having so little sense. He even told the whole heart-pounding tale of the time he was knocked out of a boat and went under and a guy whose name he did not remember saved him.

Grandpa had gotten so into the documentary project he asked us to film him giving his tour at the brickworks, which he had started running on weekends after the plant shut down in the late eighties and was named a National Historic Site. Our family had lost its stake in the factory during the Great Depression, but Grandpa was still proud his grandfather had helped create a plant that took clay from the earth and shaped it into the foundations of inhabiting and travelling life. Those bricks, he would proudly exclaim, formed the faces of famous hotels and cathedrals, lined the fireboxes of WWII warships and fashioned the launch pads for the first spaceships fired into the stars.

All told, Harriet and I shot fifty-two hours of Grandpa's stories. Never did a thing with a single second of it. I wanted more than anything for him to wake up so I could say, "I'm sorry we never got it done."

We drove out to Grandpa's place that night to pick up Link and bring him back to the apartment. On the drive, a caller on some syndicated talk radio show railed against the excesses of the time. The signs of Armageddon, he claimed, were everywhere. And I thought I saw one. It was a ball of fire from the heavens, frozen in the sky, waiting to thaw and strike the world and explode. It was a demon's egg, freshly laid and incubating in the dark. It was Remembrance Tower. The triangles of the park's logo, the yellows and pinks and reds and purples of that array of blazing lights, came into relief as we neared, took their particular forms, and then returned to a blur and disappeared in the rear-view mirror.

TOUR STOP #5: THE TRUTH

That's all for our visit to the land on which Shoahville once stood. It's time to get back to the van and head out to our next stop. Learn this as we walk, folks: neither Harriet nor I came to the park the morning of Saturday, September 13. Happy to get fired, we didn't show up for our first shifts.

Grandpa's state had improved slightly. He was unconscious but breathing on his own. Harriet tried to read Grandpa the sports page, but her phone vibrated and vibrated as call after call came through. Though it was the grand opening, and our jobs were semi-important to the park's functioning, we hadn't expected our absence would generate such a response. Harriet headed down to the cafeteria to grab some Cokes and to tell whoever was calling us from the park to kiss off. She was back fast, soda-less and out of breath.

"Shoahville didn't open," she panted. She had talked to a couple of her fellow field documentarians and Sandy, a friend in security. "Sandy said your dad showed up, gave orders not to open the park and then disappeared. I guess cars are piled up down the highway for miles and the parking lot is packed with people: actors, dancers, dignitaries, school kids, the whole shebang. No one knows what the hell is going on."

"What do you think?" I asked.

"I think we need to get out there and film."

We kissed Grandpa goodbye and promised to visit him later with an update. We headed back to the apartment to grab Harriet's camera before striking out for Shoahville.

Hold up here, folks. Before we hop in the van, you have got to know this: That was the last ride I took with Harriet. The peck on the cheek she gave me out of excitement was the last kiss we shared. She had this way of sighing when she was really frustrated that sounded like a hot iron puffing out steam. The last time I heard it was when she saw my dad's half-ton parked in front of our apartment building.

The last thing she said to me was "Let me come with you."

"I should talk to him alone" were my last words to her.

Maybe it would have worked out differently if she had protested and followed me. Maybe I wouldn't have slid into the truck but stayed outside beside her instead. Or Harriet would have made some smart remark and I wouldn't have cried when I saw my dad with this look of total desolation, like he'd seen the devil himself and learned he was the good Lord. I wouldn't have asked, "How," when he said, "Alma, the park is finished," because Harriet would have beat me to the punch and spit, "Good." But Harriet was not with me. She was in the house gathering up her camera. So instead of saying, "Tough luck," to my dad after he explained everything, I buckled up, shut the door and, if you can believe this, said, "I can help."

Harriet came barrelling out the apartment building when she heard the engine start, enraged because she thought he was stealing me. As the truck pulled away, I held my hand up to wave her away, to say, wait. To say, don't shut me out. Give me a chance to explain to you why you were just betrayed.

Dad and I visited Grandpa first. I'll leave this moment private, if you don't mind, folks. It was theirs and it will stay theirs. What I can say is that in all Dad said to Grandpa, not once did he make an excuse. He could have, you see, because what happened, folks, is that in the week leading up to the grand opening Dad had been receiving bad financial news, and with Friday's market crash Shoahville's coffers were emptied. Dad, the miracle fundraiser, had worked his tricks with the smoke of overvalued securities and the mirrors of what one expert had dubbed "financial weapons of mass destruction." That was why he had panicked in the flames and saved the diary over Grandpa. He was trying to make up for his failure. The Mikalski brothers were about to lose Shoahville, but they weren't about to lose their one, true memento.

Next, we met with the Mikalskis at the hotel where Dad had, at their request, put them up for the last two years. Over the past week, Dad had been too sick with guilt to tell them anything about the crisis. The warmth of Urban's welcome surprised me, his bright smile perfectly capping his freshly pressed suit. He quizzed Dad about his health, and asked about Grandpa, without once mentioning the park's failure to open. He even insisted the camera guy lower the lens to give Dad a hug. Zygmunt, by contrast, was a wreck. That was the first time I had seen him without a jacket. With his sleeves rolled up and his shirt soaked with continents of sweat, he looked like a D-list lounge singer who had just finished hosting back-to-back telethons. As he poured us coffee, he sucked hard at his cigarette, like he breathed nicotine instead of air, and the ash broke off into the cup he handed his brother. Urban invited us to sit on one of the leather couches in the living room. The brothers sat down on the couch opposite.

"So?" Urban said, fingering the ash out of his Styrofoam cup and eagerly watching Dad like he was a new episode of his favourite show.

Dad froze, his irises tied to his shoelaces. I asked if the guy with the camera could leave the room. Urban protested, but Zygmunt told the cameraman to wait in the bedroom. Even with just the four of us, Dad still couldn't do it.

"Imagine this," I said and pointed to the blank screen of the television.

The brothers followed my finger and watched the picture-less TV.

"Imagine we turn that on," I continued, "and we see the bad news the markets received heading into the weekend has worsened. The talking heads give way to images of employees of a once hundreds-of-billions-of-dollars-strong financial firm emptying their offices at the world headquarters, filling the streets, the prognosticators flipping us back to the time when the only solution was to choose one of those high windows and jump. Another expert, to give us a sense of the severity of the calamity, asks us to imagine the whole British Isle sinking in 1912 when her hubristic sons claimed to have built an unsinkable ship. And watching that report, you might think: 'Thank goodness I'm in the middle of the Podunk Prairies, about to open a one-of-a-kind amusement park because, honestly, why would a bunch of unpaid mortgages in the States have any effect on such an important cultural revolution on the other side of the continent?'"

I paused and Zygmunt turned from the TV to me. Urban remained swallowed by the screen.

"They *can* have an effect on what you're doing," I finished. "In fact, they've had a major effect. Along with his own shirt, Dad has lost the park's shirt, pants, underwear and a few layers of its skin."

Urban gaped from the TV to me, his mouth opening and closing like he'd forgotten his next line.

"Is there anything we can do?" Zygmunt finally asked.

"On the ride over, Dad was wondering if it might be time for you two to work your connections in Israel."

Urban made a pained noise.

"How many thousands are we talking?" Zygmunt asked.

"Thousands?" Dad gasped. "We'll need millions."

What I learned later, what we all learned, was that the day the Mikalski brothers had known would come had finally arrived: the day they had to drop their ruse and tell the truth about why they tricked my dad into building Shoahville. It's all there in the footage the cameraman shot of their conversation after Dad and I left to see Grandpa and wait for their decision.

"You think it's time," Urban said, "don't you?"

"Yes," Zygmunt replied, "it's time to show some mercy."

Now, I have a question for you, folks. Hop in the van and I'll give you something to think about on the drive to the next stop. What is mercy? How many forms does it take? Is each good? I've been trying to crack this nut for a while. There is the well-known mercy of the God who makes every move, the mercy of the God whose grace falls as randomly as the rain, the God who chose one side and then sided with the rest.

Less talked about is the mercy of the woman who buys and destroys the swastika-stamped soap the online seller guarantees was made from human beings, or the mercy of the father who comforts his weeping, bullied child by saying his tormentors are shit because of this race or that religion or such and such a class, or the mercy of the US military's top weapons theorist who, seeking a humane means of wiping out millions, conceives of a chemical compound that produces in its victims a feeling of joy one thousand times greater than high-grade ecstasy, so that even as the organs shut down and the brain dissolves their bodies cannot help but caress and kiss and copulate en masse.

There is the mercy of burning a book in an age in which it is hated, tossing it into the bonfire swollen with spines and leaves and covers, and there is the mercy of saving that book, guided by the belief that the word itself is merciful in clinging to futures and pasts that beyond that ink are exiled. There is the mercy of eyelids, which close and keep the mind from what it cannot bear; and there is the mercy of eyelids, which, closed, make the imagining mind intimate with what it missed.

Newest of all is the mercy of two comedy-activist brothers who pretended to be theme park developers for the sake of a TV pilot, *Karl and Albert Eat the Rich Across the Pond*, a follow-up to their hit UK-based hoax web series, *Karl and Albert Eat the Rich*. There is the mercy of two funnymen who were inspired to turn a ten-minute segment of a TV show pilot into a feature-length documentary when one of the oilmen/factory farmers they deceived offered to make their satirical critique real. There is the mercy of these comedians holding a press conference in London, dropping the false Polish accents, identifying themselves as Jewish Brits and asking the reporters who packed the room to tell their viewers and readers not to blame my father alone for sincerely creating this monstrous park.

He is sick, they explained, possessed by the money-grubbing, small-minded, corporate parasite that infests our times. He couldn't help but be blindly attracted to the shine of a one-of-a-kind product from a well-recognized brand, or easily hooked by a lure he was too greedy to see was fake, a bait made up of false identities, invented names and manufactured family memories and mementos, including, of course, the imaginary great-grandfather's Belzec diary – the one my dad had saved from the flames – which was a near physical replica of a concentration camp journal the brothers had seen in a museum in Laxton, but contained the meaningless markings of a language one of their assistants had concocted on the spot as he scrawled it quickly on page after page after page.

TOUR STOP #6: THE HOUSE

Zymunt and Urban Mikalski's real names were Karl and Albert Berger. My dad was their muse. His shocking willingness to "go all in" had inspired them to shoot *Shoahville: The Rise and Fall of the Big Yikes*. The Berger brothers held their "coming out" press conference in England on Sunday night, the fourteenth of September. A whole whack of studios contacted their agent. Twentieth Century Fox won the distribution rights for ten million, a back-end-heavy deal and the promise to fund a sequel. A release date in late-November was set. That would allow them to build more hype and still strike with the buzz-iron firing.

While the Berger brothers rocketed to stardom, this is where my dad stayed, right where you're standing, here at Grandpa's house. Of course, there had been furniture here then, though the place was probably as dusty and rundown as it is right now. With Harriet gone, I found a basement apartment close to the hospital and the strip mall where I ended up landing a job waitressing at a greasy spoon. The university wouldn't take me back and, truth be told, I didn't much feel like standing in front of a classroom to answer questions about Shoahville and Dad. I split my time between visiting Grandpa, waiting tables and checking in on Dad. There was Link, too, who needed more attention than Dad in his broken state could be trusted to give. I had tried calling Harriet a couple of times, but she never answered. Her voicemail recording stated: "Faithful betrayers don't need to bother leaving a message after the beep." I left messages anyway, until her number was disconnected.

Dad spent every waking hour fighting to keep possession of the park and the old farmhouse. He had let the bank foreclose on his house in the city, the new place at the lake and take ownership of all of his assets, including his investments in the tar sands and his thousands of acres of land. He called every day with updates. The goal was to open the park in December, then renovate the old house so Grandpa, who had regained consciousness but could neither speak nor walk, would have the chance to live his last days where he belonged.

Sometime in late October, Karl Berger, the brother formerly known as Urban, decided the film, *Shoahville*, needed a post–closing credits coda: an interview with Dad. Unbeknownst to me at the time, a studio rep made the offer and Dad accepted, though Dad told the guy to keep the $25,000 because he didn't need their blood money. Imagine my dad on the night before the interview, folks. The interviewer will be in this very house in less than twenty-four hours and he has nothing to show for all his work. Imagine him sitting on the porch in the crisp autumn air and watching the spot to the left of the moon where the park's logo should have shone.

I have no idea what he did that night. I wish I did. I like to imagine that I was here, and I worked the phone with him all night until dawn because we knew the light of that logo would shine again. I imagine I helped him call in favours with ancient acquaintances, crack into new leads, level with investors who have already told him to back off. I imagine I sat right here in the recliner, where Grandpa used to watch *The National* on weeknights and hockey on Saturdays, while Dad wooed each money man with the same tune: the truth and the beauty and the good of the park had survived the blast of those jokers. Shoahville was not ruined. Would the *Mona Lisa* be any less masterful if her maker was revealed to be a dung beetle? Lead followed on lead so that he barely had time to break twice to shower, the ultimate advance so close that after his second shower he remained in his towel on the phone, staring in the mirror, knowing there had to be someone who saw the possibility exactly the way he saw it.

The brother formerly known as Urban had hired Harriet to film and perform the interview. It turned out that back in August of '08, the Berger's documentary crew had brought Harriet's work to their attention, after discovering it while performing routine checks on the field documentarian hard drives. The brothers worked out a deal with her to use the opening credits from our abandoned exposé for their film. They offered her an audience that spanned the globe.

I'm the only person who ever saw the interview. The whole, uncut thing. The footage begins in Harriet's car, as she drives down the lane to Grandpa's place at 6:56 p.m. You can see the clock on the dash as she starts filming. She is alone, so everything is seen from her point of view. She parks beside Dad's half-ton and approaches the house. Light shines through every window on the main floor. The upstairs is dark. She knocks. Then she pounds and shouts my dad's name. She tries his cell and inside the house it rings and rings and rings. She tests the door and finds it unlocked. She enters.

In the house, she hustles from room to room, panning wildly, attempting to track down that ring. Search with her. Circle through here, around that, and if a few of you really want to get into it, do what she did. Call for my dad. Call, "Mr. Forge," as you follow that sound, "Mr. Forge," as you move from one over-furnished room to the next, until you finally stop at the base of these stairs and look up and see it: the telltale green of the ringing phone flashing faintly upstairs in the dark.

Ascend the stairs fast.

Sprint down the hall.

Enter this room, the bathroom, and hit the light.

Otherworldly. That's the word for it. The blast from the shotgun has slaughtered the bottom half of Dad's face. The flesh dangles in pulpy shreds like the legs of a chicken plucked and gutted. It's the shock of the stink and the unbearable colours that make you wretch. It must have happened right before you arrived, as he saw your headlights illuminate the lane, because blood still drips from the half-face to the naked thighs and between them into the toilet. For the first time, you notice the handprint he pressed in blood against his chest. It must have been his final act. There are four fingers. There is a thumb and a palm. He put them to work one last time, touching this spot right beneath his heart as if to ask, "Is this real?" Or "Hang on, old boy." Or "Go."

Say, "No," folks.

Say, "No, no, no."

Harriet sent me the disc from the camera with a sticky note that read "Only Copy." I had to find a special player to watch it. Along with the disc, the envelope came with pages and pages of letters she had written and scratched out. The tape and those letters are gone.

Let's head back to the van, folks. Just one last stop.

As we depart, here's a little food for thought: everything my father owned, that his father once owned, even that first plot his father's father's father had purchased, was taken to cover his debts. The province bought the park, shut it down for good, and tenders were submitted for the contract to demolish it. No one said boo. Shoahville employed – from construction to completion – a thousand-plus locals, but I bet you dollars to doughnuts anyone you talk to in town worked at the park for a day or two, a week at most, before quitting. The whole undertaking gave them the creeps, they'll say. It was just wrong. They knew it was doomed from the start.

Remembrance Tower was the first attraction to go. A bunch of the formerly banished protest groups gathered on the shoulder of the highway to cheer and honk their horns. I was working nights at the diner at that time so I could drive out each morning, often arriving before the bulldozers and wrecking balls and dump trucks rumbled and ripped and razed. In opposition to the protesters, who booed and heckled me, I was armed with a 20″ × 30″ sign the traffic passed too fast to see printed with my dad's face and the words *Never Forget*. We were a landmark, the dying park and me. We were a reminder to drivers they were this far into leaving or this far from returning home. The park was a tangled rise on the horizon like the claws and corpse of some giant bird of prey the machines picked clean.

Not sure if you know this, but the park is still alive online. A gentleman on one of my first tours told me so. You should look it up. I did a little research and it turns out EnjoyNet, a company formed by the park's tech team, purchased shoahville.com and changed the address to thetragickingdom. The site started out with the existing virtual ride on the RAF Sky High Flyer and the virtual tour of the Reflections on Auschwitz Hall of Mirrors, and the team poured money into creating more virtual versions of the abandoned attractions, promising a new one each month, until the whole of Shoahville was reincarnated online.

Though the virtual rides are popular, the website's real attraction is Adolf Hitler. They've made him into what they call an Artificial Intelligence Chatbot, or AIC. The AIC, programmed to respond in the written syntax and style of the Führer, draws from a store of words, facts and phrases composed of Hitler's non-xenophobic statements, five definitive histories of the Second World War and the adages of over fifty great minds ranging from Gandhi to Frantz Fanon to Mother Teresa. The idea of the thing is that Hitler is in the Führerbunker reflecting on his crimes, frozen in a moment of clarity before he took his life. In this mental state, the AIC Hitler replies to the correspondences typed by the website's visitors and sent with a single click of a mouse.

I've used the computer at the library and written in with a question or two.

Dear Adolf, what if the twentieth-century wouldn't have happened?

Dear Adolf, what if it would have?
Dear Adolf, why?
Dear Adolf,
Dear Adolf,
Dear Adolf,

TOUR STOP #7: THE EARTH

I always end the tours here, folks, way out in the middle of nothing. I'd bark at you, "Where's the park," "Find the tower," "Which way's the house," but I know we've taken too many turns and it's growing dark. When I was a runt, I loved venturing out to this hill to play make-believe, like the Russians were coming, or alien invaders, and this was the best spot to hunker down and pick them off. As I got older, I kept coming here and taking in this view while I played at a different kind of make-believe, the kind we play every day, trying to figure out what needs figuring.

What I've never thought to tell any of you who take these tours is I lost my job at the restaurant the morning I brought Link to this very spot to put him down. The manager said I would not have a job if I skipped my breakfast shift and I said I would not be a human if I left my grandpa's dog to starve to death in a heap of his own shit.

It cracks me up to think I lost a job waiting. After Shoahville was torn down, all I ever did was wait. I waited in the backyard for Link to quit circling and circling and do his business. I waited for Harriet to send word that she was going to quit movies to come home and make love. I waited for Grandpa to find his peace, or to come back, too, to pull me into that scent of peppermint and aftershave and cigarettes, plant a stubbled, sloppy kiss on my cheek and lift me off the ground and carry me to the house the way he used to, even if I was grubby from hiding in the caraganas at the end of the lane where I would wait for him all afternoon.

The morning I stole him from the hospital and brought him out here with Link, Grandpa waited, too, I suppose. He waited for some understanding of the expanse of prairie he bounced across in his wheelchair. Waited for some sense of who this woman was who wheeled him, or what she was on about stopping and laying a lump of fur on the ground at his feet, or how he was meant to hold the heavy length of metal she squeezed into his hands. He waited to understand, for something to click and resound. But he was left waiting. Consider this, folks: there wasn't a shape or a sign or a way to let him know this was his granddaughter, this was his dying dog at which she helped him aim what was the gun he had carried when the world fought the second war to end all wars.

Imagine it for a second. Together, this time. Imagine that all of us standing here are my grandpa on that morning. We're in his chair on this plain and there is nothing that says this land once sustained us, nothing that marks the billions of cells over billions of seconds we planted and raised and cut down. Nothing marks the spot a quarter mile east where we first kissed the woman who would become our wife. Or where our brother's blood spilled when the baler nearly ripped him in two. Or where the chest of the thieving hired hand broke open after Uncle Lewis shot him point-blank. Or where all that we watched fall overseas finally stayed down, the friends, the strangers, the rain and the shells and the bottle in the barracks that night we got drunk with Spence, Archie, Chick and the rest, and Stoney wouldn't let us head for town to find girls without taking our boots off first because, he asked, isn't it a marvel? Isn't it divine? The earth under the air into which we're all about to rise?

If we say, "Yes," folks.

If we say, "Wow."

Pop quiz: Would we be wrong?

HUMANITY'S WING

STANDING OUTSIDE THE HUMANITIES WING AT THE University of Toronto Scarborough, the business major doesn't have it in her to finish her essay on the building's construction. She needs to take photos instead. It's the only act that can slow her collapse under the news from three thousand kilometres southwest: later that day, in Otay Mesa, California, journalists are scheduled to snap their first official photos of the prototype border walls she never believed would be real.

Photography is the business major's true passion. The idea to hand in photos in place of an essay came to her when she discovered the man behind the CN Tower designed the Humanities Wing so that it appeared to rise naturally out of the forested ravine. Why, she wonders, can't she submit what rises naturally out of her? In Otay Mesa, the prototype walls rise to win a competition. The prize? In the words of a man she can't fathom: the right to build "an impenetrable, physical, tall, powerful, beautiful southern border wall."

As the business major continues snapping photos, and the prototypes await their official introduction, the history professor, on her way to the mailroom, stops in the fourth-floor hallway of the Humanities Wing. She takes in the wall across from her. Many of her students hate this building, calling it cold and depressing. She values the vital texture of the concrete, the way it retains signs of the workers who built it. The workers went on strike, she tells her students, delaying the opening of the campus. She invites them to notice. There's a life to it.

Down below, in a lecture hall on the main floor, the media studies professor for a course on twenty-first-century monsters attributes the proliferation of zombies in popular culture to the previous century's failure to come to terms with the Holocaust. An international development student in the back row stops taking notes. This does not resonate with what she believes. Zombies signal the west's fear of paying its debts. She raises her hand.

Beyond the Humanities Wing, on the other side of campus, a future student visiting for the first time is lost. She thinks the too-cute-not-to-talk-to boys smoking a hookah at a picnic table must be teasing when they tell her she will find the creative writing prof in humanity's wing. She tries to picture "humanity's wing" – like a bird's, a plane's, an insect's, an angel's – and then imagines how she would find the prof she is looking for inside it. She pulls out her notebook and starts a poem.

As the future student's imagination soars, the business major feels her own creative foundation waver, even as she explores the Humanities Wing's northeast stairwell, her favourite place to shoot. All the fascinating details she learned about the Humanities Wing while researching her essay – the architectural term *brutalism*, the building's multi-page spread in *LIFE* magazine, the fact that when it opened in 1965 it was the largest concrete building in the world – feel vandalized now, demolished, as though wrecked and repurposed by the prototype walls: by their brutalism, their spread against life, their record-breaking scale, stretching all the way from California to the tightening base of her aching lungs.

In the bathroom with the fly problem, the economics major scrubs his fingers after smoking a joint in the woods. He also senses a connection between Trump's wall and the Humanities Wing. Something to do with Trump's wall making a dystopian movie real in the world and so many million-dollar productions having, for real, made this building home to their fantasies, renting it to serve as everything from a post-apocalyptic prison to the headquarters of an FBI infiltrated by a cannibal. As these terrors grow in the halls and in the world beyond, he scrubs his fingers harder, not to remove the smell of weed but to buy himself time to build the will to face them.

Others in the wing – what do they build? In a main-floor study space, the psych major suffering from "fourth-year-itis" frames another procrastination-fuelled Snapchat selfie, applying the barfing rainbow filter before hurling the pic to his followers. In the margins of an essay on Spinoza, freedom and the student's decision to wear a hijab, the Philosophy TA pens, "Yes!" In an empty classroom, theatre students rehearse a gender-swapped, sci-fi adaptation of *Hamlet* they wrote for the campus one-act festival. In a new edition of Marguerite Duras's *L'amant* (*The Lover*), the professor of French literature underlines a passage, even though she has already marked that line in her two other copies of the novel, "*L'histoire de ma vie n'existe pas.*" "The story of my life doesn't exist."

The future student, no longer puzzled, enters the Humanities Wing. She is an hour late, but the professor, too preoccupied to notice, welcomes her into his office. The news of the walls took him out at the knees. He has wasted the day reading article after article about the future of the prototypes. The spin the bidders spun slapped him to the dirt. Skull stomp after skull stomp was how it felt – his inability to comprehend combined with his inability to stop searching for more.

The future student admits she is late because she was inspired after misunderstanding the building's name – humanity's wing, possessive. She pulls out her notebook and shares the poem her mishearing prompted. It's a mess, but in her mess the professor finds effort and newness and promise. He is moved to offer a few sincere words of advice and share his own Humanities Wing–related flight of fancy. Returning from the mailroom, he sometimes stops to imagine frames around different sections of his building's walls to uncover sublime paintings: an Arctic landscape captured on a moonless night; an earnest abstract; a close-up rendering of an elephant's skin, the surface concealing that massive, beating heart.

After leaving the professor's office, the future student pulls out her notebook. She takes in the wall the way the professor suggested. A form flashes down the hall, catching her eye. It's the business major taking pictures of the wall, taking picture after picture after picture after picture. The future student watches her frame and snap, frame and snap. She reaches for her pen.

On his way to the bus stop, the creative writing professor looks back at his building and, in turn, glimpses what the future student showed him. He sees it. What he needs to know could be real – humanity's wing: a home for all we build when keen to be our most probing and loving and honest and open selves. A wing that lifts us, or, as our walls and our wars and our hate and our failings blaze, a wing to escape us, to alight beyond our reach and wait for a better people, for beings who are worthy of becoming what we imagined we could become.

ACKNOWLEDGEMENTS

THANK YOU TO THE TALENTED AND DEDICATED editors, publishers, judges and programmers who previously gave the work in this collection a home and audience. Incredible people at *Eye Weekly*, *Joyland*, *Prairie Fire*, *The New Quarterly* and *The Puritan* published earlier versions of stories in this collection. Thank you to Steel Bananas Publications for producing the striking 2012 chapbook – complete with colour photos – of "Dear Adolf."

Thank you to the judges and contest organizers who recognized some of the work contained here. "What Is Missing" won *Eye Weekly*'s 2008 Short Story Contest, "1 Dog, 1 Knife" received *The Puritan*'s 2014 Thomas Morton Memorial Prize and "Humanity's Wing" was named Runner-Up for *The New Quarterly*'s 2018 Peter Hinchcliffe Fiction Award. "Year Zero" was published in *Best Canadian Essays 2014* as a work of speculative creative non-fiction. "Wave Form" won Best Experimental Short Film at the

Arizona Underground Film Festival and was nominated for Best Experimental Short Film at both the Cinema on the Bayou Film Festival and the Yorkton Film Festival. "Humanity's Wing" won an Intertoto Award at the 2020 Videodrunk Film Festival.

Thank you to the Canada Council for the Arts for the generous support, which helped get this collection off the ground.

Thank you to the brilliant friends whose advice, feedback and contributions significantly improved the works in this collection: Paola Villa Alvarez, Maria Assif, Rick Bartram, Stewart Cole, Nehal El-Hadi, Jeri English, Katie Fewster-Yan, Noor Gatih, Jim Johnstone, Lauren Kirshner, Mina Sewell Mancuso, Pascale Manning, Elizabeth Mudenyo, E Martin Nolan, Kire Paputts, Oubah Osman, Brenton Richards, Michael Trussler, Nathan Tysdal, Andrew Westoll, Catriona Wright and my fellow scribblers in C.O.W.

Thank you, Noelle Allen and Paul Vermeersch, for welcoming me to the Wolsak & Wynn and Buckrider Books family, and thank you, Paul, for your generous and stimulating editorial work. Thank you, Ashley Hisson and Jennifer Rawlinson, for the insights, talents and dedication you shared in bringing this book to life. And thank you, Michel Vrana, for the stunning design and cover.

Thank you to my family for your love, support and passion for the arts – Mom, Dad, Jayne, Nathan, Justin, Mitch, Jude, Asher, Leo and Ollie.

Thank you, Andrea Charise, for your generosity, imagination and love. Thank you for reading (rereading) and enlivening and refining the stories in this collection. Thank you for making and spinning and inspiring. Thank you for every precious second together – for the split from the program, for the laughter and feasts, for Wednesday nights (you know what that means).

DANIEL SCOTT TYSDAL is the ReLit Award–winning author of three books of poetry, the poetry textbook *The Writing Moment: A Practical Guide to Creating Poems* (Oxford University Press) and the TEDx talk "Everything You Need to Write a Poem (and How It Can Save a Life)." His short fiction has earned a number of honours, including the Thomas Morton Prize for Fiction and runner-up for the Peter Hinchcliffe Fiction Award. His short film adaptations of his stories "Humanity's Wing" and "Wave Form" have screened internationally. He teaches at the University of Toronto Scarborough.